P9-BIJ-960

THE EYE OF THE HAWK

THE EYE OF
THE HAWK

A Western Story

P. A. BECHKO

Five Star
Unity, Maine

Five Star Western
Published in conjunction with Golden West Literary Agency.

February 1998

First Edition

Five Star Standard Print Western Series.

The text of this edition is unabridged.

Set in 11 pt. Plantin by Rick Gundberg.

Printed in the United States on permanent paper.

Library of Congress Cataloging in Publication Data

Bechko, P.A.
    The eye of the hawk : a western story / P.A. Bechko. —
1st ed.
      p. cm.
    "Five star western" — T.p. verso.
    ISBN 0-7862-0991-7 (HC : alk. paper)
    I. Title.
PS3552.E24E95   1998
  813´.54—dc21   97-38393

THE EYE OF THE HAWK

A Western Story

Chapter One

The thunder rolled, a hollow, mournful rumble filling the fathomless night sky. Rain slashed downward out of the darkness, glinting silver and gold where it passed before a lantern swaying gently beneath the overhang.

He stood there, sheltered by the paddle wheeler's verandah-style roof, gazing out across the black, oily-looking waters of the churning Mississippi. He drew deeply on his hand-rolled cigarette. The wind accompanying the storm slapped him in the face with water droplets and set about curling and tousling his shaggy, black hair. Steel glinted in the depths of his blue eyes, and he allowed his emotions to be swept away by the power of the storm.

A friendly poker game had broken out in the parlor after dinner, and he had joined in for a while, leaving after winning several hands to seek the easy comfort of his brocade smoking jacket and to take a turn around the deck before retiring. He leaned one broad, thickly-muscled shoulder against the wall and waited. What he waited for, or why, even he wasn't certain.

Water sloshed violently against the hull of the river boat as the storm continued to rage, lightning slicing across the belly of the heavens in jagged tears. For an instant, the swollen, black clouds seemed near the point of bursting, so filled with brilliant white light they could not quite contain it. Then the light would ebb, and the cycle began again. Water, falling from the sky, would become a shower of diamonds, and again the thunder shuddered its way through the paddle wheeler from stem to stern.

The river boat's interior was quiet, its occupants riding out the storm, for the most part, snug in their state rooms. Nature's fury hesitated, as if to draw a deeper breath. *Slap, slap* came the sound of the broad, flat blades of the paddle wheel breaking water against the churning river, now filling the void left by the thunder's pause. Let the rest of them huddle in their safe nests. He had always loved the raw savagery of a full-blown storm.

Stepping forward, he leaned on the banister, turning his face to the slashing force of the rain, flicking the remnants of his cigarette into the river. Something moved very near him, and he half swung around, cursing his inattention when the gunshot, both ear-splitting and head-splitting, exploded, the slug ripping into the side of his skull in a momentary flash of blinding pain. The force of its impact sent him spinning along the rail. His own momentum sent him over the side and into the frothing waters of the muddy river.

Rona Burr swung down off the driver's box of the freight wagon in a manner like she'd been doing it all her life, and that would not be far from the truth. Ever since her father had started the line, when she had been no more than a little bitty thing, she had climbed all over the coaches and the heavy freight wagons, harnessing horses, doing some of the packing, seeing to the tying down of a load. There wasn't much she had not done over the years, including keeping the books and riding the big wagons with Hank, her older brother.

"Hank! We better get it moving if we want to pull out on schedule!" Rona took a couple of wide, unlady-like strides toward the office. "Hank!?"

"I'm comin', I'm comin'!"

Hank burst through the door, shotgun gripped in his hand,

red hair blazing in the sun, long legs swinging in ground-eating strides. He grinned broadly when he came up alongside her.

"Keep your shirt on, li'l sister, five or ten minutes one way or another ain't gonna mean nothin'."

"It does when you promise a timely delivery," Rona differed. "You see anything of Tyler?"

Hank shook his head.

"If he isn't here in five minutes, I'll drive myself." Rona wasn't making an empty threat. She had done it often times before.

"We've got a stage due in here in about two hours," Hank reminded her, green eyes gentle as they rested on his feisty little sister. "You know you can't just take off on a freight run right now. I'll go alone, if Tyler doesn't show."

Rona planted her hands on denim-clad hips. "Damn! How can he be so good and so irresponsible all at the same time? And you can't go alone. It's too risky."

"Rona, we've been short-handed since Pa died, and it ain't likely to change any time soon. If we want to keep the Burr Line running, we're going to have to take some chances."

"We're going to keep the line running all right, and I don't care what it takes."

"Glad you feel that way, Rona, 'cause I decided we needed some help."

"Help?"

"The line is being attacked, if you can't see it. We're losing drivers, passengers . . . and we're bleedin' money like a stuck hog."

"But, what kind of help?"

"You ain't that dense."

"I don't know, Hank."

" 'Course you don't. That's why I sent for him."

"Him?"

"A fella I met some time back. He don't come cheap, and he'll be collectin' a shootist's wages, but with him up on that box for a few trips it's gonna stop. I wrote him. Ain't no reason to think he won't be here any day."

She hesitated, looking past her brother's shoulder. "Here comes Tyler now. We better talk about this later."

Hank nodded his agreement.

Tyler Harding approached on legs bowed enough to be wheels themselves. His floppy felt hat was crammed down on his head over a balding spot, allowing his thin, brown hair to trail from beneath. Piercing black eyes darted from brother to sister and back.

"Ready to pull out?"

The question was directed at Hank more than Rona, though Tyler had learned through experience that the woman was just as likely to be driving the team as her brother. Even before their pa had passed on a few months ago, she had taken a hand in almost every aspect of the line. Not good as far as Tyler was concerned, but there it was.

Rona broke down and smiled. Tyler could be trying at times, but he was dependable. He'd stuck before their father had died and the first of the trouble had begun. He stayed now, despite the fact they were being hit repeatedly by thieves and desperadoes, and it was beginning to take on the appearance of some sort of personal vendetta being waged against the Burr Line. Passengers were becoming scarce, and some of their smaller shipping contracts were in danger.

"Let's roll." Hank climbed up on the wagon, propping the butt of the shotgun against his boot. "Don't hold dinner for us, sugar, we're gonna be a spell."

Tyler swung up beside Hank, stowing his weapon beneath the seat and taking up the lines to the three braces of horses strung out before them.

"Don't you listen to him. We're gonna make record time," Tyler's gravelly voice roared the promise, and he lifted the lines, slapping them down over the horses' backs. "*Hiya!* Gee up thar!"

The team of six, sturdy draft horses leaned into their traces, and the wagon rumbled off, gaining speed as it hit the outskirts of town.

Rona sighed, not taking her eyes off them as they disappeared into the distance, wishing she was on board. A little wistfully, she watched the dust curling upward in a thick, concealing plume behind the wagon as it lumbered out of sight. Then she squared her shoulders and strode back into the office. There was a lot there needing her attention, and Hank had been right. One of their coaches was due in soon. The only question, as far as she was concerned, was whether it would actually arrive or not. The door slammed behind her with pistol-crack loudness, and her boot heels rang solidly against the plank flooring before she dropped into a high-backed chair behind the desk.

Her father's chair. Memories of the past flooded her. She could still feel his presence when she sat in that chair. She rubbed her palms gently over the oiled, walnut arms of the chair in a loving caress. God, how she missed him. She knew Hank did as well. They had been a close family.

"Well, Pop," she said into the comfortable silence of the empty room, "what do you think? That stage gonna make it in all right?"

She could almost see him propping worn, muddied boots on the edge of his desk, creaking back in this chair, and giving the matter proper consideration over a cup of steaming, black coffee. Then he'd flash her a broad, big-toothed grin. " 'Course it will, tad," he'd say, annoying her with one of his favorite nicknames for her, "it'll be all right. Burr Line'll

11

be here long after we ain't."

The memory brought the sting of unshed tears to her eyes. Fighting to retain control over what threatened to dissolve into a cascade of tears, she sank back deeper into the chair.

"It isn't fair, Pa, it just isn't!" Rona complained in a taut voice to the empty room — empty save for *his* presence.

"Never meant to be," she could hear him answer, as if he were really right in the room with her and not dead and gone, lost to the cold waters of the river when the lumbering freight wagon had overturned, pinning him beneath. "Don't cry for me, li'l girl," he would say. "You got troubles enough of yer own."

The creak of the old chair, the feel of the wooden arms beneath her palms, the smell of the leather, made him seem alive. Alive as before the accident. Closing her eyes, she felt again his warm presence permeating the room.

Joseph Burr had never had much patience for self-pity or anything else that stopped a man — or a woman — from just getting up and having at it. He'd raised two kids and built a business on his own. Never married again after his Riana had died of the fever, claiming he didn't intend having a stranger raise his kids. So, for more than twelve years, he had done the job himself. That and almost everything else that came along.

The thought of how much he had given them, of how much he had sacrificed over the years, brought a lump to her throat now. All that . . . only to have it end for him alone in a cold river, drowning in water only halfway up the freight wagon's wheel.

Now it was only herself and Hank. That thought sent the patter of fear racing up her spine on the icy feet of fate. Dear God, what would she do if anything happened to Hank?

"Now you're borrowin' trouble, li'l girl." She tried out her father's words, but they rang hollow in her ears.

She wasn't borrowing anything. They already had their plates full of trouble. She felt a heavy weight press against her chest. She thought about the information Hank had imparted to her about his having sent for someone. A man good with a gun. Maybe her brother was right. Maybe it was the only way. She straightened in the chair, squaring her shoulders. No, not maybe — it *was* the only way.

"Stage comin' in!" a rough, masculine voice bellowed from outside.

Rona jumped and looked at the clock. She couldn't believe how much time had elapsed, and she had not touched pen to paper or opened a single ledger. She left the chair with a bounce that sent it spinning into the wall behind and bolted out the door. Her heart was pounding and would not quiet until she saw the stage with her own eyes, saw for herself it was unscathed.

But what she saw first was Sam Reo. The sight of him froze her in her tracks. The chill emanating from him had the bite of a January frost. His cold, slate-gray eyes rested on her a moment, then slid off to other things. She shuddered, then also looked away, fixing her gaze on the approaching coach, trying to shake off the apprehension Reo's presence triggered. If he was here, at least the coach had to be safe. Reo had had a hand in their troubles. She was as sure of that as the sunrise of the coming day.

On heavy, rocking springs the coach drew up in front of the office, and the driver jumped down from one side, the shotgun from the other.

"Quiet ride, Miss Rona," the driver offered before striding off toward the saloon to cut the dust from his throat with a beer.

She nodded absently. No doubt it had been. Sam Reo was right here in Stillwater.

Chapter Two

The air was cold and clawed at his throat as Torregrossa sucked it deeply into his lungs in a primitive instinct for survival just before he hit the surface of the roiling waters. The river was even colder. The shock of it was all that kept him conscious. The awareness of it was all his mind would hold onto as he sank into the murky depths, while the paddle wheel driving the boat barely missed his head. The same instinct that had caused him to inhale as he struck the surface had him clutching at the last threads of consciousness, knowing that to slip into darkness now would mean certain death. Slugging along in rhythm to his heartbeat, the blinding pain in his head gave him a focal point. Holding his breath made it worse and magnified the sensation of his brain smacking against the inside of his skull.

He ordered his limbs to move, to fight for the surface, and they began to respond. Feebly at first, still dazed by the enveloping cloud of pain, he moved upward. Then with more vigor, and finally, in wild frenzy, he strove for the fresh air above, pulling water like it was rocks on a hillside, all the while praying that he would be able to make it before his tortured lungs burst. His ascent to the water's surface was like a man climbing a mountain. First one hand reached out, grasped the water, pulled it to him, and then the other. With a final lunge, he broke through, gasping and sucking fresh air into his lungs. He floundered a few moments, certain he was going to sink again, but the same driving force that had not let him slip into eternal sleep took over again. The dark shadow of the shore loomed closer than he had dared hope. The mind rebelled, muscles protested, but leaden limbs spontaneously began to function, dragging him through the liquid that dragged at him seemingly like mud. There was no decision involved as he managed to keep swimming, bringing the shore closer with each short stroke across the river's current.

It was the core of the man, the soul, that would not stop fighting. Ethan Torregrossa was not one to die easily. If he were to meet death, it would be while fighting for life. Survival came first.

The soft, slippery floor of the river bottom at last brushed against his knees and elbows. He planted his hands in it, dragging himself up against the pull of the water, digging his knees in against the drag of the current. Blindly he had continued to swim, even when the water had become shallow enough for him to have walked upright. Still, even now, he had not the strength to climb to his feet. He swayed where he was, stymied, determined not to collapse into the water, yet unable to move forward, until a cold slap of water washed across his face once again.

He groaned, gagged on the water threatening to choke him, then, on hands and knees, pressed forward, dimly aware that he was near his goal. Dry land and the chance for rest were only a short distance in front of him. Waves of frigid blackness were washing over him as he struggled the last few feet forward and caved in on the riverbank. His legs were still sprawled half in the water, and his cheek rested in the ooze of the river mud. Disoriented, something nagged at him to keep moving, to find shelter, to protect himself, but where he fell was as far as he got. The broad expanse of the Mississippi slid silently past him where he lay.

Torregrossa had not seen the three men rush to the rail of the big river boat after the slug that had nearly taken along a piece of his skull had sent him plunging into the river's icy grip. Neither had he seen them standing at the ready, guns in hands, waiting for him to surface, nor finally disappearing back inside when they had seen no further sign of him and armed river-boat men appeared on the deck of the paddle wheeler.

Consciousness returned with a deep, dull, pulsating beat, pressing against the inside of his head. It felt as though his skull were bulging outward, grossly distended from the rest of him, despite the cooling pack of mud that it lay upon. With an effort that made sweat pop out instantly along the length of his body, Ethan managed to gather up himself enough to roll to his knees. He gagged, swayed, and began to take stock of his situation. Leaning a little forward toward the water, dizzy and confused, he reached up to touch the source of his misery. Instantly a stab of white hot pain flashed through his head, traversing it side to side in a sword-like slashing that made him feel that the top of his head was no longer attached. He dropped his hand, blinking furiously, trying to clear his vision. Gently, he splashed some water on the wound, hissing from behind clenched teeth and squeezing his eyes tightly shut in denial.

Wet and half-dried mud clung to most of him and caked blood coated the side of his face, his neck, and part of his shoulder. He was stiff all over, though his only wound was the one that had creased his skull. How long, he wondered, had he been unconscious? There was no way to tell, except for the wound, and it was fresh. Very fresh. Dimly, he remembered the boat and his swim ashore. It had to have happened on the boat, though he could not recall what had occurred. Would whoever had shot him figure him for dead? Why had he been shot? For an instant he felt a cold wave of panic rippling through him as he swayed unsteadily on his knees close to the water's edge. He could not remember his own name, let alone the identity of some other, or others, who had tried to kill him for some equally unknown reason. Now, he couldn't even remember in which direction the boat he had been on had been heading. *Up river or down?*

The moment passed, and he attempted to focus on the problem at hand. Whoever had shot him could be coming after him. He had to have shelter, and he had to do something about the wound soon. He stood up. It was like being socked in the belly by a grizzly. He opened his left eye, and his vision instantly blurred. His stomach heaved against his insides, and he retched helplessly before stumbling, half doubled over, for the sheltering brush.

Once upright and moving, his stomach settled down some. His head felt like it been jarred loose from its once firm seat at the top of his neck. But it was better to be moving than standing still, feeling the icy cold of his panic worming its way past all his defenses. Weak and sick, Ethan stumbled through the brush, casting about for a good spot in which to hole up for the night.

Carried on by his own momentum and the one-track set of his mind, he reached a fallen log close beside a thicket of bushes, the branches reaching out to form a canopy between the slender trunks of the brush and the old log. His good eye had picked it out easily enough. *Was it something he was practiced at?* He let go of the thought. At the moment it made his head throb all the more to try and remember anything. Carefully he eased himself down between the log and brush, the branches softly swishing overhead as they swung back into place. An instant later he lost consciousness again.

Rona Burr stepped out on the porch in front of the stage office, looking for some sign of the return of the freight wagon.

She didn't know why, but she stood there on the wooden planks, one hand on the rail, the other on her hip, staring apprehensively up the dusty street, waiting. There was plenty to keep her busy inside, but here she stood. A dark sense of foreboding surged through her. She held her breath until lack of oxygen forced her to draw air deeply into her lungs.

Then she saw Tyler Harding riding slowly down the street astride one of the stout draft horses and leading another. There was no thunderous rumbling of turning wheels, no thick plume of dust rising behind him, only the sharp *clip-clop* of hoofs being put down by heavy animals. The sound grew. Rona started in Tyler's direction, first walking, then jogging, and finally running. When she spotted a limp form draped over the back of the second horse, her heart began pounding in an irregular rhythm, echoing in her ears. She recognized the shape slung over the other plodding horse's back.

Dear God, it's Hank!

Rona wanted to scream. Thoughts flew through her head. *Was he alive? Please be alive! He couldn't be dead. I have to be strong. Mustn't allow Hank to see my fear.*

She reached Tyler, hazel eyes flicking from her brother's still form to Tyler's round, open face so obviously filled with pain.

"I'm sorry Miss Rona, he's hurt real bad."

"Hurt?"

Tyler gave a start. "He wasn't dead when I pulled him from the wagon. He didn't . . . ?"

Rona was running her hand over her brother's hard, angled face, fingers scuttling over his throat with the energy of a fleeing spider, feeling for a heartbeat, sighing with relief when she felt the faint flutter.

"No. No, he's alive, Tyler. Help me get him inside."

The freight wagon driver slid from his broad-backed mount,

18

jumping to help Rona ease her burly brother from the horse's back, plainly amazed the man was still alive.

"Call the doctor!" Rona yelled at the various townspeople who were grouping closer now, drawn by curiosity. "Hold on, Hank," she ordered and pleaded in the same tone at her brother as she and Harding carried him between them to the stage office. "Don't you dare die on me! Just hold on. We're gonna help you."

As they edged through the door, Rona strained every muscle she possessed to keep from dropping her brother's legs. With a quick movement, she jerked her head in the direction of the table where they sometimes fed stage passengers.

"Put him down there."

Between them they eased him down as gently as they could. His face was bloody, his arms cut and bloodied, and his clothes full of sweat, mud, and more blood. Rona began frantically tugging at Hank's shirt, opening it to the waist, staring down at her brother's battered chest.

"What happened?"

Tyler fell back a step. "Ain't exactly sure. Somebody set a trap. Couldn't've been nothin' else."

Rona got some water, rags, and bandages.

"Why couldn't it have been anything else? Dammit! Tell me what happened."

She was mopping frantically at his torso now, trying to wash away enough of the dirt and blood to assess clearly her brother's injuries when Stillwater's doctor hurried through the door. She paused in her endeavors when she saw him.

Doc Riley set his bag on the table beside Hank's head and pulled off his jacket. "Just keep on with what you're doing," he snapped in Rona's direction, then hurried to the washstand near the door, scrubbing his hands with the strong, lye soap on the stand.

Rona did as Doc Riley requested while looking up again at Tyler. "You still haven't told me what happened."

The driver had moved a little closer to the door, plainly uncomfortable. "We came around the bend up near Sand Hill. Never realized how blind that turn is till today. We were movin' at a pretty good clip . . . horses weren't half tired. Ol' Hank, he was laughin', givin' 'em some head, an' this tree comes slidin' down the slope like the devil himself pushed it. Took the wagon in the front wheel, splintered it right then and there. The wagon collapsed, and the horses panicked. Hank tried to hold 'em instead of jumpin'. I tried to help him, but it went over too fast. I was thrown clear, but Hank got pinned under the wagon. I'm just grateful all the horses weren't killed. Otherwise I couldn't've never got him back here a-tall."

"Sweet Mary," the doctor murmured once he stepped up to where Hank lay sprawled on the table.

The words were barely out of his mouth when Hank began wheezing, the scratchy, whistling sound piercing in the weighty silence of the stage office.

Doc Riley compressed his lips and shook his head.

"Don't you go givin' up on me!" Rona demanded in a fierce tone, but her lips quivered.

The doctor explored the injured man's body with sensitive, trained fingers, finding one broken bone after another. He laid his ear against Hank's chest and looked more worried than ever.

"We're gonna try, Rona, but this don't look good. I'd advise you to have the preacher here in case."

She put her hands on either side of her brother's face and looked down into the pain-wracked visage. "Fight. Do you hear me, big brother? Don't you listen to him. Fight!"

Hank's green eyes rolled open, unfocused, dim, lacking in awareness, yet Rona could see something of him in their depths.

Some part of Hank was there, hanging on, but if that presence faded, she would lose him. She was sure of it.

The wheezing got worse rapidly until it sounded like her brother was gasping for breath just beneath the surface of some water. His eyes rolled, focused on Rona above him, and stayed. She smiled, a tremulous, reassuring curve of the lips.

"Better get something under him and raise his head so he can breathe," Doc Riley said gruffly, his observation an order directed toward Harding.

The injured man was beginning to struggle, eyes wild and fixed on Rona even as he drew ragged breath into blood-swamped lungs. His bloodied lips worked hard to form words, and Rona gently wiped them clean with a dampened cloth.

"Save your strength," she said softly. "The doc's going to help you."

Hank's head rolled from side to side in denial. "Rona . . . Tyler . . . don't trust. . . ."

"Who? Who shouldn't we trust?"

"No" — barely a pained whisper — "no."

He was thrashing again. His body straining, his breath a hoarse, tearing sound in their ears as Rona and Stillwater's doctor tried to quiet him. Hank stiffened, gagged, and choked. Riley frantically tried to clear his airway, but Rona was aware acutely the very instant her brother ceased to struggle. The moment his breath caught, the silence, like the scattered pieces of a puzzle come together, became complete.

Doc Riley shook his head sadly and passed the back of a hand, stained with Hank's blood, across his sweaty forehead.

"I'm sorry, Rona. He's gone."

Rona, her brother's red-haired head cradled between her hands, just stared. The shock was too deep. She couldn't feel anything, couldn't cry. Her breath caught high up in her chest, and her throat was suddenly raw with the effort it took to draw another. She looked down into his now peaceful face and moved her hands away, then turned to Tyler Harding.

"Who is it he didn't want us to trust? Did he know who did this?" she choked out.

"I don't know. I didn't see nothin'." Harding's thick, wax-stiffened mustache twitched as he answered the question. "We was just talkin' about Sam Reo before it happened."

"Don't go jumping to any conclusions," Doc Riley cautioned Rona. "Sam's held in high esteem by many in these parts. Just 'cause they were talkin' about him don't. . . ."

Rona stepped away from the table, chin raised, wild, mahogany-colored hair an aureole about her face. "My brother is dead, and I'm going to find out who's responsible. After that, I'll kill whoever it is. I swear it."

Chapter Three

The sound was distant and annoying. It repeated itself time and again — a low, wrenching sound, almost a groan. *Where could it be coming from?* Fragmentary consciousness was deceiving — reality mixed up with a dream state. He was sure he would awaken in his bunk on the paddle wheeler at any second, that this was a very bad dream.

But when Ethan Torregrossa opened his eyes, he was not on the boat. He felt like hell and weak as a dragged cat. Worse, the sounds he had been trying to decipher had been coming from him — not a promising thing for survival if someone were looking for him.

Full awareness put a stop to the croaking groans, and with the return of cognizance came a realization that he had made it through the night. Morning was spilling its golden glow, the sunshine pouring down through the canopy of leaves in soft dapples and glistening on the river behind him. He lay quietly, not eager to move his head now that the pain had died down to a distant, if persistent, throb. The pain was a reminder of the wound that had put him here. Memories were elusive. Any attempt to put thoughts together in a coherent sequence was impossible. So he focused on the wound instead. He had to do something about it, clean it, bandage it somehow, or his brains were likely to leak out on the Mississippi mud.

He sat up slowly. His head swam at first, but steadied down as did the rolling in his stomach. There remained the problem with his vision that would not go away. Sight from his left eye was still blurry, almost to the point of being useless. That realization made his gut clench. Then, he remembered the night past. *There had been voices and the sound of horses nearby.* Or, had he only dreamed it? Hallucinated it in some nightmare dream state of anxiety? He couldn't be certain, but he could be cautious. With skill long ago learned and now utilized through habit that could not be blotted out with loss of memory, his good eye swept the area for signs of trouble, finding nothing out of place.

Thirst, abruptly making itself known, forced him to ease himself over the disintegrating log and make his way back to the river. Clothes still clammy from his midnight dunking, Torregrossa dropped to his knees in the soft mud of the river bank and drank. The cool grittiness slid down his throat like ambrosia, the chilly wetness of it a soothing balm.

It was a long time before he sat back, reaching automatically to his throat for the neckerchief he had assumed would be there. But it was not, and for the first time he took notice of the clothes, clinging to his body, as something other than soggy rags. There was not much for him to see. He was wearing boots of superior quality, a pair of pants, black in color and of a good material, and a dark green smoking jacket trimmed in black. What had he expected? Another puzzle. What *should* he have been wearing? There was no gun and no holster buckled about his hips, no shirt beneath the smoking jacket, and no neckerchief around his neck. Confused, he started going through his own pockets as he would search a suspicious stranger's. He did not come up with much for his trouble.

"Who are you?" he asked himself, anxiety beginning to color his tone.

He found some mushy tobacco and papers for cigarettes in a leather pouch, a good, gold pocket watch, ruined by its dunking in the river, and the elusive neckerchief his fingers had instinctively sought. Happy to find at least that much that was familiar to him, he withdrew the square of material from his pocket, surprised by its weight. Then he saw the reason for it. The neckerchief formed a small bundle, tied up at the four corners. Eagerly he fumbled with the damp knots, cursing stiff fingers, finally untying them.

Several twenty-dollar gold pieces dropped heavily into his hand. A wad of folding money, thick enough to plug a hole the size of his fist, and an envelope folded into a small, fat square remained in the folds of the neckerchief. The money, though it appeared to be a large sum, was not what held his interest. Absently he stuffed the money back into his pocket and started eagerly unfolding the envelope. It was just about as wet as paper could be without disintegrating into shreds, and the name was smeared and streaked almost beyond legibility. On the envelope itself, he could make out only the words **New Orleans** in the address, and that was more guess work from the loops and scratches remaining than from being able to decipher the blurred ink. Carefully he pulled out the single folded sheet of paper from the envelope. He could, with much effort, make out a couple of the words in the short letter. They did not make much sense out of context. But standing out clearly within the smear of ink against white paper, as if it were meant for him to see, was the name of another town. **Still-water**. Refolding the paper, he carefully tucked it in his pocket. It was all the clue he had.

Rinsing out his neckerchief in the swiftly flowing stream of the river's current, he proceeded to bathe the wound along the side of his head, carefully washing away the caked blood and mud before tying the neckerchief, folded into a triangle, around his head. He glanced down at the smooth surface of the river's eddy and saw dark, brooding eyes returning his gaze. Having done this, he no longer felt the face reflected in the waters was that of a stranger.

Ethan Torregrossa sat back on his heels and looked out across the racing river. He had something more now than what he had awakened with. The names of two towns. New Orleans and Stillwater. Neither stood out prominently in memory, but either could be a home or a destination. Both, he felt, were somehow significant. Where would he be recognized? More importantly, did he *want* to be recognized? It was logical to assume that whoever had tried to kill him would try again, if he was found to be alive. If and when that happened, his life could depend on spotting whoever it was first. It became quickly clear, even to his befuddled mind, that it was difficult to make a decision with nothing to base it on. It was there, everything he needed, right below the surface, just out of reach. He would remember, in time, but, for the moment, he didn't even know where the hell he was.

There was only the river. Yet, even in his haze, there was one thing he did know. It was important that he move. He drank frequently, consuming large amounts of water while he paced the riverbank, regaining his equilibrium and pondering what his next move would be. He was consumed by an undeniable urge to turn west, away from the river, and wander out into the wilderness. It was an illogical, impractical impulse, yet one that held him in its grip. Was it an old desire, deeply buried, working its way to the surface like an old splinter ready to be removed? He sat down for a moment, knowing his faculties were not functioning properly, aware that he must come to some kind of decision.

Reasoning power won out over impulse. He had no horse, no gun, and no immediate prospects of acquiring either. All he had were the clothes on his back, the money in his pocket, and the soggy, unreadable letter. With sudden decisiveness he settled for following the river. At least, he would have no trouble finding the water he craved like an alcoholic thirsted for his next drink. He did not allow himself to question his decision, but stood up and started to walk. Upstream. No doubts assailed him about whether upstream or down was the correct direction. He would turn west when he was properly outfitted. Perhaps by then his memory would reassemble itself and his thought processes would be clarified.

Her eyes burning with unshed tears, Rona Burr brushed the dirt from her hands and stood back from the grave, watching quietly while two stout men earned their money, filling in the dirt over Hank's casket. She didn't feel much of anything — only numbness. She was far too weary and perceived herself as very much alone. Those who had attended Hank's funeral were already scattering, returning to their daily routines, but she remained, watching and listening.

The first few shovel loads of dirt hit the wooden casket with a loud, hollow sound. Now it was a continual dull thumping, and even that was dimming to a fainter drub — earth softly colliding with earth, as the hole rapidly filled.

"Miss Rona, I don't think it's good for you to be a-standin' here, watchin' this," Tyler said, placing a tentative hand on her arm.

"Well, I do."

"You can't bring 'im back."

"I can say good bye properly."

"Don't reckon Hank'd care for this."

"Right now, what he would have wanted doesn't mean a lot," Rona snapped, lips stiff, words sharp. "It's what *I* want, what *I* need. And if he can see me from wherever he is, and it makes him mad, then he can damn' well just *be* mad. I'm mad. Madder than I've ever been in my life. He left me alone to run Burr Stage and Freight, and it's going to take me a while to forgive him for that."

"You ain't makin' much sense."

"I don't care."

The gravediggers finished their work, neatly mounding the soil over the grave, then turned, tipping their hats to Rona before they walked away.

Tyler Harding stared at Rona who continued to stand, immobile, beside the fresh grave of her brother. He had never seen Rona this way. She had been strong, always in possession of herself, always the one to do the prodding and pushing. Today was different. She hadn't broken down outwardly, but there was something different about her. A crumbling of defenses. He decided he was going to stick around for a spell. He stepped back, giving her room to be alone.

"Ty, I'll understand if you want to leave Burr Line after this. You can draw your pay as soon as we get back to the office."

"You firin' me, Miss Rona?"

For the first time since the service had started at the graveside, Rona shifted her gaze from the disturbed earth beneath which her brother now lay.

"No."

"You givin' up on Burr Freight and Stage Line?"

She stiffened. "No, certainly not. I'll run it myself if I have to."

"Then I'll be stayin', if you still want me."

Her face softened. "Thank you, Tyler. I appreciate it. I know Hank would, too."

"Like you said, don't much matter what Hank would've liked now that he's gone. I'll be takin' my orders from you."

Rona smiled faintly, feeling intensely the pain of separation. Hank was being set aside already, removed from their lives, from *her* life. So soon and she was being forced to relegate his flashing, green eyes and stubborn, red-headed nature to the past. He would not be there to help her again. He would not be there to offer gruff advice. From this time on, he was alive only in her memory.

A lump formed in her chest, one she had staved off until that moment, and tears filled her eyes, though she refused to allow them to spill out. "We have work to do," she said thickly.

Her heart cried out to her lost brother, but she turned, stiffening her spine, and walked away.

Chapter Four

Miles passed slowly for Ethan Torregrossa, the severity of his head wound forcing him to stop and rest often. Nonetheless, he was gaining in strength and surprising himself with his knowledge of what plants could be eaten and which herbs were good medicine for his wound. He was certain one day soon the memories that remained just beyond his reach would surface, and his life would all come flooding back. He believed it firmly. The key, he had decided, lay in taking each minute, each day, as it came. In time, the wound on his scalp would heal, and so would whatever damage had been done. However, doubts erupted when he contemplated the injury done to his sight. Vision from his left eye was nearly non-existent, the dimness not receding. Instead, the blurring seemed to have worsened, initiating the frightening thought of permanent half blindness. *What will happen to a man like me if I'm half blind?* The thought, and the fear it instilled, caught him by surprise. Somewhere in his brain he knew who he was, but he did not have access to that information, except when a fleeting, random hint of himself like this slipped through. *What sort of man am I that the thought of parietal blindness would cause such an overwhelming dread?*

No revelation was forthcoming, but he could not take his attention away from the problem of his eye. Perhaps, he reasoned, if it were not required to do its job, if it had a chance to rest, it might recover. He settled for shifting the neckerchief bandage so that it covered the bad eye as well as the wound.

He continued to walk, following the river. In the absence of any other weapon, he had broken off a slender limb from a tree and sharpened one end down to a point by sanding it against a rough rock. It came in handy for spearing fat fish in the shallows and for grubbing various roots of which he appeared to have knowledge. At least, he was eating whenever his belly bit against his backbone with ferocity.

As he walked, he gnawed on a tuber dug up with his makeshift spear, chewing until he had most of the moisture and pulp from the plant. Throwing away the tough, woody remains, he pressed on, rounding a sharp curve with something less than a cat's silence. Around the curve he ran smack into the twin barrels of a shotgun. *That* jolted a memory: another time, another place, a weapon identical to this pointed toward him, the roar of the gun, his own amazing, god-damned luck as he had dived clear, picking up only a couple of stray pellets. For an instant all he could see were those two barrels pointed in the general direction of his midsection. With these types of guns, the general vicinity was close enough.

He froze. Then his good eye locked with icy, gray ones sunk in the wizened face of an old geezer behind the shotgun. The grizzled man, eyes glittering from beneath bushy, gray eyebrows, stared first at the green smoking jacket, then at the bandanna bandage wrapped around the injured man's head.

"Where the devil you come from? I sure didn't ask for no comp'ny," he rasped in a guttural slur that somehow wanted to take on the tang of the South. "You're almighty dandified to be roaming around these parts."

The last comment didn't seem to warrant an answer, so Ethan stayed put and held his tongue.

"Got a name?" the feisty old-timer prodded, while watching the younger man closely for reaction to his abrasive remarks.

Steel was in the depths of the one, clear, blue eye not covered by the man's bandanna, though it would not be so apparent now as it would be when the stranger was aroused. There was a straight, powerful set to his broad shoulders that stiffened at the shotgun-wielder's questioning, a weathered look about his skin as the area about his right eye tightened. When the old man glanced down at the stranger's clothes, he spotted a shiny patch on the hip of his pants where a holster had worn the cloth.

"Hawk," the name escaped inexplicably from Ethan's lips, and then came a flash of the name painted on the side of the paddle wheeler — the *River Hawk*. His own name had nearly surfaced when he had spit out the alias. He was certain it had been very close, about to break through the veil. He convinced himself it did not matter for the moment. It was for the best he keep his true name to himself until it all came back. Until he knew whom he could trust.

"Put that shotgun down. You can see I'm not armed."

"Can see it," the wily fellow agreed, "but don't rightly believe it. Can't understand a man of your cut not goin' heeled." He peered steadily at Hawk a bit longer.

"Who the hell are you?" Hawk demanded.

"Folks call me Arkansas Billy," he growled with rooster pride. "Run a ferry landing on the river. Got me a tradin' post and stage stop a short ways from here. Looks like you've got yerself some trouble."

All his life Billy had prided himself on his ability to read men. It was, he swore, this unique talent to be right about people almost all of the time that had kept him alive so long. He read no threat in this man, only a strange kind of emptiness he had never before come across. It was just a feeling rather than anything the dark stranger had said, for he had not said a whole lot.

"Some," the younger man agreed. "We in Arkansas?"

"Huh? Arkansas? You mean you don't *know?*"

Hawk grinned a little, quickly deciding to throw in enough of the truth so as to cause less suspicion. "I managed to fall off a river boat. Don't exactly know where I ended up."

"Looks more to me like you was throwed off," Billy returned, "but you guessed right. This here is Arkansas. How long since you and that river boat parted company?"

"Few days."

Billy nodded, allowing the shotgun to ease down into a more comfortable carrying position. "Well, reckon you could do with some grub better'n you prob'ly been eatin'. An' mebbe a good night's sleep. Come with me back to my place, and I'll see you get both. Might even come up with an ol' shirt you kin wear."

Billy set a brisk pace. Hawk had no trouble keeping up, but he realized he was unusually tired by the time they reached the cabin perched above the river. The cabin was quite a sight. It was no shack, standing straight, and appearing solid enough to withstand even the flood waters of the Mississippi. Scattered around the outside were various items from Billy's inventory such as wagon wheels, what looked like some rough axles, barrels, crates, and hundreds of smaller items neatly stacked. A couple of horses, three mules, and a milk cow shared pasture in a fenced-in area along the riverbank.

"Sit yerself down an make yerself to home," Billy said cheerily, throwing open the door to the cabin and trotting inside. "Can't let a prospective customer stand around half dead on his feet." Billy rolled the words out of his mouth as if they were tumbling around a handful of pebbles.

Inside, Billy sloshed a drink of whiskey into a dull glass, handed it to Hawk, then got to cutting thick slabs of bread from a loaf.

"Grub and drink are on the house. Anythin' else you'll have to pay fer."

Tossing off Billy's liquor, Hawk felt it burn all the way down and suspected it to be from Billy's private stock — probably even his own private recipe. He moved a box of odds and ends — mostly sewing needs and tin cups — off a chair and sat down, setting his empty glass on an exposed square of table.

The inside of the cabin was much the same as the outside. It was neat, everything tidily stacked, but completely cluttered with goods Billy bought, sold, and traded. Barrels of flour and beans lined the walls with smaller kegs of salt, sugar, and coffee stacked alongside. Several bolts of calico were lined up in a corner, flanked by bottles of whiskey and boxes of ammunition for almost every weapon known to the frontier. Coal-oil lamps hung from the ceiling in a neat row. Scores of candles resided in boxes such as the one he had moved to make room to sit down. A couple of rifles hung on the wall. Near the door a six-gun in its holster caught Ethan's eye.

"Like it?" Billy asked, following his gaze. "I have a couple others layin' around, but that's the best of the lot." He gave Hawk an appraising look. "Might be too rich for you though, considering your condition, I mean."

"How much?" Hawk asked, remembering the money in his pocket.

"Twenty dollars. Just got it in a couple of days back myself. Wondered how long it'd take you to get to it." He stared at the shiny spot on Hawk's pants where a holster had been. "Didn't figure you fer a man to go unarmed fer long. Take it down and try it."

Hawk lifted the holster off the nail and flipped the belt around his hips, buckling it in place. The holster slid down over the slick spot on the side of his pants, and his hand dropped naturally to the gun butt with an easy drift. He tipped the gun out of the holster at hip height, handling the weapon with a natural, well-acquainted ease.

Billy didn't appear in the least surprised by his guest's expert handling of the weapon. It appeared he was a well-oiled machine. Hawk was not surprised, either. Despite holes as large as train tunnels in his memory, just touching the pistol triggered his automatic response. It was as though a spark had jumped from the gun to his hand, sending a surge of energy through him, rekindling waning confidence. He recognized a part of himself, but didn't know where it fit in with the rest of the jigsaw puzzle.

Holstering the gun again, Hawk pulled out one of the three wads into which he had separated his money. He handed Billy the twenty dollars without argument, then handed him another couple of dollars for a supply of bullets.

The size of that bankroll drew a low, soft whistle from Billy. "*Whooeee*," he said, holding his hand out for the money. "Good thing I'm an honest man. Plenty of others around who'd blow you in two fer a whole lot less'n that."

"Been tried before," Hawk declared, and no sooner than the words were out of his mouth, he knew them to have been true even before the bullet that had sent him tumbling from the deck of the *River Hawk*.

"Cain't argue that," Billy said, eyeing him closely.

The weapon had transformed the stranger. He no longer appeared half dressed. He was more relaxed, and an air of completeness hung about him. It was almost a swagger, yet it was not that of a prideful man or a cruel one. It was on a much deeper level, one that Billy could not fathom — that of a man who's lost himself and has begun to come back.

"I'm going to need an outfit," Hawk interrupted Billy's thoughts. "Everything for the trail, and a horse if one of yours is for sale."

Something had changed, shifted, and Hawk knew he wouldn't be wandering any longer. He was heading west.

"Sure thing," Billy agreed amiably, serving up a mess of hot beans, cold beef, bread, and steaming coffee. "The sorrel is mine, but you can have the black. I'll give yuh a good deal."

"He any good?" Hawk asked as he tore into the meal with all the vigor of a half-starved man. "Not that I'm in a position to quibble."

"Ain't the best," Billy answered honestly, "but he's a fer cry from the worst I ever seen."

The ferryman's guest polished off the meal, washing it down with several cups of hot, black coffee. "Like to take a look at that black now," he said, rising, feeling much stronger for the food in his belly.

By the time they finished their business, Hawk had a horse and old battered saddle, a sack of grub for the trail, canteen, a hat, and had discarded the tattered smoking jacket for a plaid shirt. Since he had strapped it on, the gun had not left his side. Until that moment he had not been aware of just how naked he had felt without one. He planned a bout of target shooting just as soon as he was far from Billy and the cabin. Until then, all he had to go on was a hunch he was mighty good.

Night was settling in, and they returned to the cabin. Billy got to starting a fire and lighting a couple of coal-oil lamps, while Hawk busied himself tying his purchases into an easily manageable bundle.

"I thank you for your hospitality, Billy. I'll be pulling out in the morning."

36

"Figured as much." Billy squinted in Hawk's direction. "You're figurin' to find someone. I can read it in your eyes."

The old man had no way of knowing how close to the truth he had struck. Hawk was planning on finding someone all right, and that someone was himself.

"Well," Billy went on, "mebbe you do. I don't rightly know. But you better let me bandage that wound proper if you're set on lightin' out come mornin'."

Hawk touched the dried, crusty bandanna he had employed as a bandage since he had come to on the riverbank. The pain in his head had faded to a dull, distant roar, except when he turned too fast. That brought a crashing wave of dizziness washing over him.

"I'd be obliged, Billy."

Billy proved himself to be a pretty fair country doctor.

"Wound's healin' already," Billy announced, finishing his work. "No thanks to you, leavin' it all stopped up with dirt, which I reckon proves that, aside from nearly gettin' your brains blowed out, you're one healthy son. Still, you cain't leave everything to luck."

Hawk agreed, and, when he slept that night, his gun remained near his hand. It was the first night he slept through since falling into the river.

Chapter Five

Rona stared pensively out the window at the sun-splashed street and tried to focus her thoughts on what she should do. After her brother's funeral she had hired a driver, and he had lasted the better part of two weeks, making a couple of clean runs before he'd been shot — fortunately not fatally — and quit. Now it was just herself, Tyler, and an old-timer who took turns holding the ribbons of the stage. The old fellow hung on because he had too much plain mule-stubbornness to call it quits. She rubbed her temples and sighed. How could she let an old man keep taking those kinds of risks? Before all this trouble he had helped in the office and occasionally manned a freight wagon. Nothing in this country was entirely without risk, but this . . . ?

"He's got more sand'n he knows what to do with," Ty Harding announced as Manning brought the stage in safely one more time. "Everything's fine," he added hastily.

She jumped up from behind the desk and darted out through the door with Ty dogging her footsteps. Despite Ty's assurance, she was apprehensive when she lifted her eyes to the battered, dusty stage, rolling in — Jake Manning driving, outfitted in loose, filthy clothes and a hat with the brim flattened back above his piercing dark eyes. His rifle was propped beside his foot, barrel pointed skyward, just like it had been when he had left. But something was different, something about the way he held himself. Rona peered intently at the old man, the awful fear of seeing injury squeezing her chest. But that concern was unfounded. No injured man could have jumped as sprightly from the driver's seat as he did.

"Clean run, Miss Rona," Jake called out as his heels hit the dust of the street. "Didn't like it none, though." He spat tobacco juice in the dirt, directing it politely away from her feet. "Spotted that Reo fella more'n a couple of times."

"Where?"

"Ridin' alongside, keeping his distance."

Tyler opened the stage door for the single passenger, allowing a young, nattily dressed young man to climb out, heading directly for the nearest saloon.

"He didn't try anything?"

Her driver shook his head. "Naw." He grinned through tobacco-stained mustache and beard. "Reckon he was scairt of me. I'm tough as old gristle and more'n a mouthful to chew. Probably figured he'd wait for the next fella."

He cast Ty a meaningful glance, making it apparent to Rona that his opinion of Tyler Harding was something less than complimentary. Rona ignored the comment. From the very beginning Jake had not gotten along with Tyler. She couldn't fathom why.

"I'll get the team," Ty said with good humor, ignoring old Jake's cutting remark. He quickly unharnessed the horses, fingers nimble with experience, but he couldn't conceal completely his apprehension from Rona when he glanced up and down the street as if he half expected to see Sam Reo, riding in bold as brass at any minute to gun them all down.

Rona frowned. *It was Reo, it had to be . . . didn't it?* Things had gone rapidly from bad to worse shortly after his arrival in Stillwater. Yet, plenty of townspeople seemed to love him, or at least respect and admire him. Rona shared none of these feelings for Reo. Instead, she watched and listened. If she ever got proof that Reo was responsible for her brother's death and the troubles of the Burr Line, she would kill him herself.

A good horse beneath him, supplies in a sack tied to the saddle horn, and a battered old hat pulled low over the bandage encircling his head, Hawk turned due west when he left Arkansas Billy's trading post on the river. He was sure the answers he was seeking lay in that direction. It was an odd feeling. Something like the migrating geese must feel to draw them safely home. He rode like he had been born to it, easy in the saddle, and the black moved beneath him with a smooth, silken gait. The cayuse, he decided before he had covered very many miles, was a better horse than Billy had given him credit for being.

Days passed quickly. Hawk felt comfortable riding the lonely trails, seeing no one. Memories were his only companions, and they were an unpredictable lot. There were sequences, bits and pieces. Unconnected episodes, some violent, others pleasant, wandered unhindered through the uncluttered passages of his mind.

In his frustration he pushed on relentlessly, westward, not knowing exactly what he was looking for, yet certain he would recognize it when he saw it. It seemed like his mount was tireless, though he, at times, felt the fatigue of many hours in the saddle. The blurring and darkening in his left eye had not lessened, but he was adjusting, living with it day to day. He compensated, allowing for the half blindness on his left. His marksmanship was honed to a fine edge, and he rarely missed his target, even while hunting and the target was on a dead run.

Living off the land, it seemed, was as natural for him as his next breath. He might be more than just a fast gun, but there was no doubt in his mind, now, that he was that. Possibly a

40

known gun as well, and it was this potential that kept him from seeking out settlements.

Painfully aware of the gaps in his memory before he had been wounded, Hawk was now also plagued by dreams. Disjointed fragments, chunks of a life lived in different places, at a different time. Many of his waking hours were spent puzzling over them, trying to grasp the thread that would unravel the tightly woven tapestry of his memory.

The black moved quietly and at a steady pace beneath him. If he had not been deep in thought, as he had been many times over the past days, he would have sensed trouble sooner. But, distracted, he barely avoided stepping right into the middle of it. The sound of low, angry voices reached his ears before several men and horses hove into view as he rounded the base of a low hill. Hidden by the roll of the land, the men had not yet spotted him, but Hawk saw in an instant that they were set on a hanging. At the center of their attention was a boy. Slender and not very tall, the brown-haired kid was soft of face despite the flash of anger and hatred in his eyes. His hands were bound behind his back, a rough hand on his arm forcing him to sit his horse very straight while the makeshift noose dangled before him.

From the moment he saw the youngster, he knew he was not going to let them hang the boy. With nothing to guide him, no experience readily available, Hawk drew on instinct. Without thinking, his hand dropped to his gun, checking to be sure it would slide easily from the holster. Things had already gone too far for gentle persuasion. Only a show of force could stop what was happening in an uncannily familiar situation. Muscles tense and palms dry, Hawk let his horse keep walking, approaching the knot of men with the cool deliberation of one who was aware of exactly what he was riding into.

In fact, he knew too well, he reflected grimly. There were four guns, and he was standing alone. The realization hit him like a jolt. He swayed in the saddle, then nearly froze, swept by the chill of the simple knowledge that he had *always* stood alone. Knowledge, not conjecture. He had craved no companionship, sought none . . . until now. Irritably the thought was brushed aside. Now was not the time.

He surveyed the scene as his pony's hoofs, clacking sharply against stone, took him closer to the men surrounding the boy. They turned toward him, and, once he had their attention, he did not pause, but kept on coming, steel-blue eyes dark and challenging.

"How old are you, boy?" Hawk directed his question toward the kid, his words slicing the tense silence despite their soft, Southern bevel.

"Sixteen," the youngster replied breathlessly.

He was scared green, a wonder he could draw in enough air to speak, but it was obvious the kid had plenty of sand.

The youth sized up Hawk as he moved in steadily, and a flicker of hope enlivened his muddy-brown eyes. He perked up considerably, looking around for a way out. No way of telling what the stranger's position would be in all this, but his presence might provide a distraction, a chance to run. He sized up Ansel, the hateful old man his mother had saddled him with as a stepfather, and figured this might give him his only chance, and he wasn't going to blow it.

"This ain't none a your damn' business," the old man, stiff and sour of face, snapped at Hawk. "Clear out before we figure you for the kid's partner."

"Maybe I am," Hawk replied with a tight smile. "What then?"

"We'll string you up with him!"

42

Hawk, battered and trail weary, wasn't wearing the look of a man who would back down.

"Don't I know you from somewheres?" a stocky, beak-nosed man piped up, eyeing the interloper with a steady, penetrating gaze that would have made most men squirm. "Mariposa, maybe? Man with your looks had himself a real rep as a fast gun."

"What the hell?" the older man exploded. "This ain't old home week. We got business to tend to, so let's get on with it. Hoist him up, Grady!"

"I wouldn't do that, Grady," Hawk countermanded the older man's order in a soft tone that stopped the stocky, little man cold. Then he reached for the bridle of the boy's horse as Grady reached for the noose dangling in front of the kid's face.

The other men, who had remained quiet, looked uneasy, shifting in their saddles. Tough and callous, they were hardened men, but they hadn't counted on a complication like this. One hand resting on the bridle of the kid's horse, the stranger kept his right hand free and near the butt of his pistol, while it appeared he controlled his own horse with nothing but his legs. And he was calm as the eye of a storm, almost inviting them to try gunning him. The men shared the same thought. Was he that fast, or that stupid? The aura about him promised it was far more likely to be the former than the latter.

"Grady," the old man grated, "do as I say."

Still Grady hesitated, uncomfortably occupying the position into which the situation had put him. But, aware of the fury the old man could conjure, he stretched his hand toward the noose again.

This time a gun appeared in the stranger's hand as if by magic. Its muzzle, however, pointed not in Grady's direction but toward the old man.

Lips stiff, they barely moved when Hawk spoke. "I wouldn't," he countermanded the old man's orders a second time.

With red-faced rage the silver-haired man confronted the barrel of Hawk's gun, not the least bit intimidated by it.

"The boy's a horse thief, and I'm gonna see him hang. Right now!"

Hawk didn't release the bridle or adjust his position. His gun remained pointed casually over his saddle horn toward the ring leader.

"You steal a horse?" was the question he directed at the youth.

"Well, hell, you damn' well don't expect him to admit it, do you?" the old man demanded.

Hawk shrugged, and then confusion broke loose. The boy's horse spooked and jumped like a jackrabbit, bolting with enough wild ferocity to tear the bridle from his hand.

There wasn't enough time for that cayuse to get a running start, and a gun cracked sharply almost at the same instant the animal sprang forward. The kid dropped out of the saddle like a sack of grain.

Hawk silently cursed his half blindness that hadn't let him see that coming. He slid to the side of his nervous horse, clung there a moment, and fired as guns turned in his direction. One man tumbled off the back of his horse with a low grunt. Hawk hit the ground and threw himself to the side, rolling as bullets snapped on all sides, then scrambled for the boy, moving fast, uncertain as to whether he was alive or dead.

A searing, white pain tore into his shoulder when he landed on top of the boy. He groaned, not knowing why he'd thrown himself over the boy and taken the slug meant for him. His reflexes had responded as if it were the kind of

44

thing he did every day, and in another instant he had blocked his mind to the shock of the pain and dragged the kid's limp form clear of the line of fire.

Hunched up behind a clutch of large rocks, the youngster was sprawled behind him on the ground. Hawk sized up the situation. They were out there, three of them at any rate, and they were after the kid's hide. Now his own was included, and they'd already gotten a piece of it. He winced when he touched the new, raw, and bloody wound in his shoulder. It wasn't very serious compared to that of his companion who lay unmoving, hands still tied behind his back. They had to make tracks and find some place to lay up and tend their hurts. How badly the boy was injured Hawk had no way of knowing, but he fervently hoped the kid wouldn't die after all he had just gone through to help him.

He lobbed a couple of shots toward some scrub brush and rocks where he figured the remains of the hanging party to be holed up. He was rewarded by a sharp yelp from the area where he had been aiming. Hit or startled by the bullet's nearness, the man had given himself away. The others were clustered in close proximity to that one.

Hawk spotted the boy's horse, standing near some scrub, reins dangling on the ground, ears flicking nervously from side to side each time the guns cut loose. His own black mount was only a few feet back from where Hawk and the boy lay. The horses were not clearly visible to the men intent on the kid's hide, and he had no intention of killing the three men if it could be avoided. He snapped off a few more shots, pinning them where they were. They were wary of his gun, and he pressed this advantage. Later, a lot would depend on how determined they would be to track the boy down.

Quicker than hell could scorch a feather, Hawk holstered his gun, maneuvered the boy up into the saddle, then vaulted easily on behind him. He grabbed the black's reins and then, in passing, grabbed the reins of the boy's horse, took out at a walk, then a few strides farther on lifted the horses to a brisk trot, finally to a full gallop. He rode with a grim set to his lean frame and the glint of blue steel in his eyes. The boy's heart fluttered against the back of his hand where he held it across the kid to keep him from falling out of the saddle. It was fast and faint, and Hawk brought out the wadded-up handkerchief he still carried, stuffing it tightly against the wound to slow the bleeding. He held it there, teeth gritted against the throbbing of his own shoulder. There was no more he could do. They could not stop longer than to change horses frequently, giving each animal a rest in its turn from the double load, hoping to put many miles between themselves and pursuit.

Instinctively Hawk concealed their tracks, splashing up streams, keeping to the hard ground, avoiding areas where their passage might be marked by a broken twig or some crushed grass. The kid remained unconscious in the saddle before him, and his gut told him they'd lost the lynch party when they crested a low rise, coming out on a long flat pointing the way to some high hills rolling due west. He touched his heels to the horse beneath him and headed that way.

Sam Reo rode into Stillwater like a potentate. He was alone, a heavily built man, solid, with no fat on his frame, square of feature and dark of skin, the center of attention with his rust-colored, straw hair, cutting an imposing figure as he rode down the street. He barely took notice of anyone near him, but gave the impression he was well aware of everything and everyone. His slate-gray eyes were flat, yet penetrating, and few cared to meet his direct gaze.

Yet, when Rona Burr looked at him, she did not flinch. Indeed, her usually sparkling hazel eyes locked onto him, bore into him, and searched his hollow shell for some remnants of a soul. She crossed the street dead in his path, glancing up defiantly as if daring him to run her down. Sam puzzled over her, thinking about her more often than he cared to admit. She was in the way, and so was the Burr Line.

Rona slowed her pace, lifted her chin, and looked up at the man on horseback. "Haven't seen you in town for a few days," she remarked acidly. "Something keeping you busy?"

Reo froze, eyes sweeping the street, searching for something, or someone. "I go where my business takes me."

"Business? You look at land, but you don't buy or settle. You ask what it takes to run the Burr Line, but you don't make any offer, although you insist you're considering a business to invest in."

"Do you think the Burr Line would be a good investment . . . now?"

Rona colored, answering through stiff lips. "Of course. It's not unusual to have some hard times."

Reo chuckled, the sound dry as wind-swept autumn leaves.

Her anger rose. "Maybe Stillwater just isn't the place for you."

"You don't think so?"

"Not particularly."

"Same could be said of you. You've got more troubles than ticks on a hound, Miss Rona."

He emphasized the *Miss* until it sounded like something foul in his mouth. Then he touched the brim of his hat, guided his horse around her, and continued down the street without looking back.

Rona stared after him, less than satisfied with the encounter. She wanted to yell, accuse, demand explanations, but she had done none of that. Proof. She needed proof, or the whole town would turn on her. Somehow she had to find out what Sam Reo hoped to gain by the continued harassment of the Burr Line.

Chapter Six

Hawk checked the horses where he had picketed them in a position that would sound the alarm if someone were to approach the hidden camp, then lumbered back to the fire. And lumbering was exactly how he felt. He sure hoped to hell he wasn't going to see any more trouble any time soon.

The fire was burning low, and that was the way he wanted it. He had made do with the supplies in his canvas sack instead of hunting meat or scouring the surrounding countryside for edible plants. Neither he nor the kid were any too mobile. His meager meal of hardtack, jerky, and coffee had been consumed in gulps and snatches, between tending the boy's wound and jumping up each time he stirred.

"Son-of-a-bitch in a sack," Hawk hissed when he finally took a moment to work loose the makeshift bandage he'd slapped over his own shoulder wound.

The fabric had dried tightly into the wound, crusting over and causing the cloth to rip away what little protection it had offered. The pain was toe-curling, but Hawk forced himself to make sure the bullet had gone through, the process dousing him in his own sweat. He then cleaned it and covered it with a more substantial bandage.

His own injury was bad, but it was his left shoulder and would not interfere much with the mobility of his right side if he needed to move fast. The kid's wound was a lot worse. Hawk glanced in the unconscious boy's direction, wondering why the youngster was so important to him.

"Hell, kid," he muttered into the glowing embers. "You die on me, and I'm not even gonna know what to scratch into a marker. Guess we've got that in common. No name. No past, and no future. Only the here and now."

He heaved himself up and threw another blanket over the boy, a couple more sticks on the fire to keep it alive, and took the horse blanket for himself, huddling down into it as he propped himself up against his saddle. There wasn't much hope for sleep this night.

Yet, there was difference between him and the kid — if the kid lived — in what lay ahead in the morning. If his patient woke up, everything would be as it had been for him. His past would return. Not so for Hawk. He never knew what surprise lay around the corner of the next dawn. Might he even wake up his former self? Would he remember the kid with the dawn? He stretched his legs out, slumped down, and closed his eyes, determined to catch a few winks before the next small noise woke him.

Decked out in sturdy canvas pants, a thick, brown, home-spun shirt, and a floppy, black, felt hat, Rona climbed up on the seat of the freight wagon, donning a pair of buckskin gloves so well used they were molded into permanent curves.

"You sure you want to ride the freight? Told you I'd be plumb tickled to take this one up them hills for you." Jake fixed her with his piercing eyes, then turned his head and spat tobacco juice into the dust.

"I'll be fine, Jake."

"I dunno."

"Any problem with the horses? The wagon? The set of the freight?"

"Hell, no! I seen to all that myself."

50

"Then you've done your job for this run." She glanced at the sun, barely beginning to show over the tops of the eastern hills. "I'll be back by nightfall. Karl's place isn't that far."

Jake frowned.

Rona relented just a little. "Don't worry so much, Jake. This shipment isn't worth stealing. Just a few odds and ends Karl needs. Won't amount to much, but the line can use all the cash it can get now."

"Still don't like it."

"You don't have to."

Rona smiled, picked up the leather lines, and snapped them sharply over the horses' backs. "Move it out, boys. We don't have all day!"

The horses, fresh and rested, danced in their harnesses, leaning into them, taking the wagon forward with a lurch and rumble. A little eager to get moving herself, Rona leaned forward on the seat, lifting the horses to an even trot as she gave Jake a short wave and rolled out of town, leaving him behind in a cloud of dust.

"You watch yerself, you hear!" Jake yelled into the rising cloud of dust.

Already out of earshot above the low thunder of the big wagon, Rona did not acknowledge Jake's admonition, but she had every intention of doing just that, as evidenced by the heavy, double-barreled shotgun stowed beneath her seat and the rifle propped beside her knee.

With the coming of a new day, the burden Hawk had taken upon himself seemed improved. He had not slept longer than an hour at a time, only rest snatched in short drifts into the semi-aware state of half sleep. He had been rewarded when the golden wash of the morning sun spilled over the rocks, and he could see the kid's breathing was easier and that there

51

was some color in his cheeks.

His injured shoulder stiff and radiating that awkwardness to other parts of his body, Hawk climbed to his feet and forced movement. He restoked the fire, setting the coffee pot on the still warm coals, then stepped over to the boy to inspect the wound in his lower back. It hadn't been easy digging the bullet out, and, to his relief, it had not bled much during the night. With the rising of the sun, the injured youth's chances of survival went up considerably.

Satisfied, the gunman with the devil's hand went to move the horses to better graze. In the dark of night he had chosen their campsite well. It was a moot question whether he had managed it by accident or some prior experience that had come to the fore. Whichever, their little hollow was well sheltered from sight, and the horses had not so much as whickered in the night. Hawk moved them to a patch of brush and sparse grass closer to the camp, pondering the position he and the kid shared. They weren't going to be moving from that place any time soon. He would have little difficulty staying awake during the day in spite of his lack of sleep. It would not be until night fell again that it would catch up with him. By then, he would either have to come up with a way to warn himself in case of trouble, or risk a deep sleep without it. The last thought did not much appeal to him.

On the way back to camp, he came across some plants he recognized to possess healing roots and pulled enough for the boy's wound as well as his own. It took a few minutes for him to pound the tubers into a soft, pulpy mass, using a couple of large rocks. Then he moved his own bandage aside, applying some to the raw wound, front and back. Next he administered to the boy's wound. As he worked, the soothing coolness of the roots had started to ease the stiff soreness of his own injured shoulder. Instinctively he knew it would be good for a fever as well, and, while the kid hadn't pitched one yet, that was certainly big on the list of future possibilities.

The boy's dressing replaced, Hawk rocked back on his heels. He was easing the kid down again onto the blanket when he felt the boy stir beneath his hand. The boy's eyes blinked open for a few moments, appearing glazed, but then they cleared, and he was staring up into Hawk's eyes.

"Thought sure I was gonna wake up dead," the youth whispered dryly, then asked groggily: "You kill 'em all?"

Hawk shook his head. "You were hurt too bad for me to stand and fight even if I had wanted to, which" — he added — "I didn't."

"How far'd we get?"

"Far enough," Hawk answered with a bravado he didn't feel. "What's your name, son?" He offered the canteen to the boy's lips to cut the dust.

The boy swallowed and coughed shallowly, then responded. "Danny Mil . . . Harper. Who should I say saved my bacon back there?"

"Hawk."

"Suits you." He took another pull on the canteen, appearing to gain strength even from that small luxury. "You took a helluva chance back there, bailin' me out. You sure must go huntin' it."

Hawk gave Danny a stern look. "You have any kin I can send you to when you can travel?"

"You just met all the kin I got left yesterday."

The gunman gave the kid a puzzled look.

"Man who tried to lynch me was my pa. Well, my stepfather, and considerin' what you did for me, I reckon it's only fair I tell you I stole that horse to get me as far away from him as I could ride."

"You better get some rest." Hawk said, cutting Danny off.

"I'll need you to keep your eyes open later for a couple hours so I can snatch some shut-eye."

"Give me a gun. I'll take my turn. I ain't about to have that old man come riding up on us unexpected." That much said, he eased back on his blankets and closed his eyes again.

Hawk then backed off to throw some jerky into a pot of water to make some broth. He contemplated Danny, a boy, just becoming a man. He could get himself into a lot of trouble before he finally made it — *if* he did. At a time when he recognized his own raw vulnerability, he spotted the same in the kid. *What am I going to do with him?* he asked himself. He was still too much a boy to be running around wild country alone. He lacked experience, a potentially deadly shortcoming. Just as deadly could be teaming up with him. If someone was after Hawk, intent on murder, Danny would be as much a target as Hawk was himself. The situation, either way, made for an unpredictable and dangerous future.

True to his word, Danny stood watch a couple of hours that night while Hawk caught some badly needed, uninterrupted sleep.

Chapter Seven

Days passed swiftly. Hawk was perched on a good-size rock, staring off to the southeast. He kept his eye on the open country they had traversed a few days before, having now reassembled his six-gun after cleaning and oiling it and loading cartridges into the empty chambers. The two of them were healing, and Hawk felt fit, bits and pieces of his memory returning, and more at ease with himself than he had been since he had taken the plunge from the river boat. But both of them had itches that needed to be scratched. They needed to be away from here, and the urge to move west was still on him even though there was no sign of pursuit by the boy's stepfather and the rest of the lynching party. The question of what to do about the kid still nagged at him.

Abruptly Hawk froze. An odd, scuffing sound off to his vulnerable left side sent him flying off the rock, landing on one knee in the dirt as he wheeled, gun cocked, and ready. Confronting him with cool calm was Danny. Easing the hammer of the six-gun back into place, Hawk sighed as he regained first his feet and then his position on the rock.

"Don't ever do that again. You just about got your head blown off."

"Been standin' there a couple of minutes. You didn't know I was there till I scraped my boots in the dirt. You're half blind, ain't you?"

Much as Hawk hated to admit it, even to himself, that was

the way things stacked up. He no longer saw anything out of his left eye except a dim, hazy blur. Whoever those fellows had been on the boat, they had done a job on him, something he would surely remember when the time came, and he was sure that time would come.

"Did it occur to you to just ask?"

"It's somethin' a man might grease the truth about, and I had to know for sure one way or another, if I'm gonna be ridin' with you."

"Don't remember passing out any invitations."

"Neither did I," Danny retorted, "but I was sure glad when you showed up without one. One of these days you'll have reason to think the same. Besides, I've been fit enough to leave for a couple of days. If you were planning on parting company with me, you would've ridden out by now."

Danny had him there.

"What I was planning on was getting you to some town somewhere and on a stage."

"To where? I already told you I don't have any kin. What's the point, anyway? I don't figure on droppin' myself in on strangers."

"Look's like we're in the same boat, kid, and I've got trouble dogging my trail. How do you think I got this bad eye?"

"Makes us even, don't it? You think those fellas who were tryin' to stretch my neck will give up? Once we start moving again, there'll be a trail for 'em to follow. Only reason they ain't caught up already is you're about as crafty as an old fox."

Hawk shook his head and gave Danny a grin out of one side of his mouth. "All right, son, you win. For now. We'll give it a try for a while and see how it works out."

Clasping his new friend's hand, the kid grinned, eyes lighting up. "Partners," he said enthusiastically.

"Partners," Hawk agreed, accepting the boy's firm handshake.

Rona saw him, and more than once, as she guided the freight wagon up the old mountain road. The rutted trail could be treacherous, but Rona knew it well, a veteran of many climbs while her father had still been running the Burr Line.

She looked around for some new sign of Sam Reo as she rounded a tight curve and began another steep ascent. There was no trace of the man now. Nothing. She didn't glimpse him, but she figured he had a couple of hardcases working for him. Her hand wandered to the sleek, cool barrel of the rifle propped beside her knee, gloved hand hovering near it as the team trudged on. Her eyes narrowed, lips pursed in concentration. She was alone again. She could feel the emptiness of the mountainside, the undisturbed caress of the air.

Karl Schmidt's place was only a couple of miles farther on. She was going to keep her word to Jake. As soon as she arrived, she'd help Karl unload and start back right away. She sighed deeply. There was little that could scare her, but she felt a chill of fear run up her forearms now, and for that, too, she cursed Sam Reo's name.

Danny had a lot of pride, plenty of guts, and handled a rifle with a deft accuracy that would have drawn open admiration from almost any man on the frontier. Hawk observed with interest when the kid took to riding just off his left side. At first he had been annoyed, but as they rode together, and the boy began to show what he was made of, it set easier with the man, having him there.

"That wound on your forehead is fresh healed," Danny observed as they moved along at a steady pace.

"That's right."

"You reckon that eye's about as good as it's gonna get?"

"I reckon."

Hawk surprised himself with his direct answer to Danny. He had come to accept it. The eye was as good as lost, and the fear that had earlier clutched at his insides with icy fingers was gone. Left in its place was a reservoir of calm and the deep-seated realization that he would have to be as good, or better, than he had been in the past — or die. It was that simple. He had no idea if his enemies were close or even what they looked like, at least not in so many conscious thoughts.

"Like my daddy always said, root hog or die. I don't intend to die."

Danny laughed. "You ain't a man likely to fail livin' up to your intentions. Your daddy sounds like a man who took to life head on."

"He did," Hawk mused without thinking. "But he wasn't a very strong man, and his main weakness was his wife."

"Your ma."

"No."

"Oh, I see."

Hawk didn't see himself, so how could the kid? *Where had that memory come from? Was it comparable to the stray droplet of water from the hole in the dike before the dam burst?*

They rode on in companionable silence, putting miles behind them with a hard-driving desire to get clear of what was pursuing them both. While the boy covered his blind side, the gunman focused on keeping the kid's hide whole, pushing them on even after prudence would have bid them stop.

They camped one night, after long days on the trail, outside a little town near the Texas-New Mexico border. They were running short on supplies. Eating with Danny was like sharing a meal with a winter-starved lobo who was possessed additionally of a hollow leg.

"I'll go on into town and get what we'll need," Hawk announced when Danny had already unsaddled his horse and gathered wood for the evening fire. "You aren't healed enough to be taking any chances yet."

"An' who's gonna watch out for you?"

Hawk hardened, steel glinting in the depths of his good eye.

"All right, all right." Danny backed off in a hurry. "I'll put the coffee on. Figure you'll be back before it boils."

"You figure right."

Hawk made the trip in what seemed to him to be record time. His visit to the general store was brief, including only enough jawing with the storekeeper to keep any thoughts of a suspicious nature from that worthy's mind. Having left the town without having taken the time so much as to have a drink to cut the dust, Hawk made his way back to camp with alacrity. He reined his horse in sharply when he approached, spotting the fire burning higher than was usual with Danny in charge. The camp stood out like the black clouds of a dust storm in a bright day, and that made the tiny hairs at the back of his neck stand up. He smelled trouble just as surely as if the air was perfumed with the bloom of the honeysuckle of his youth. It was unnaturally quiet. No sounds of night critters, no song of insects, no halloo from Danny. He stared into the darkness. His vision, which in the past had been like that of a cat, failed him now. The annoying blur in his bad eye combined with the darkness made him unsure of what he was looking at.

He waited. He had not heard any shots, upon his approach, and in the clear air they would have carried a good distance, so he did not think the boy dead — at least not yet. Hawk drew a deep breath and let it out slowly. Old instincts were stirring. Below the level of conscious thought plans of action

59

were being drawn and discarded. Enemies were nearby, and he knew he had to move because he was in the open. Were they Danny's enemies, or his own? It didn't matter. He wouldn't abandon Danny, and that meant he was going to go at this head on, crashing into the middle like a wild Texas longhorn.

"Danny!" Hawk called out in genial greeting. "It's me. I'm comin' in."

The distinct click of a gun hammer being drawn back filled the following silence. Then a low, muffled response from a voice, a stranger attempting to sound enough like Danny to draw him into the camp, was the belated reply to Hawk's hail. He touched his heels to his horse and rode into camp like he had swallowed the bait whole. Head held high, the black stepped out smartly, and chaos broke loose inside the camp.

"Sheeeit!" That was Danny.

A scuffle ensued, boots scraping against hardpan, followed by the unmistakable thump of a body hitting hard and a gun cracking sharply at close quarters. Orange flame flared from a gun barrel, the discharge near the ground.

Hawk's six-gun filled his hand in an instant as he jumped clear of his horse, slamming into the ground with bruising force. An instant later he was gathered into a half crouch, gun leveled on a phantom outline just beyond campfire light, a darker shadow against the inky blackness of the night surrounding them.

"Hold it!" Hawk snapped, voice flat and menacing. "Drop the gun!"

The stranger jerked, startled, then half turned, shifting the muzzle of his gun in Hawk's direction and snapping off a shot. Despite the speed of what happened, Hawk had time to wonder if the man were alone, or if he was facing more than one gun. He dropped flat and rolled, coming up on his belly, elbows propped against hard ground, his gun answering the fire of the first. For an instant in time gun thunder rolled, then, abruptly, silence settled again over the camp.

"You got 'im!" Danny exclaimed hoarsely from the darkness beyond the gunman's vision.

"Any more?" Hawk barked the question, then instantly rolled to another location in anticipation of hot lead, heading in his direction.

"Naw, just a lone gun."

Cautiously the older man climbed to his feet and went to check the fallen man, gun still in his hand. Whoever he was, he wasn't a threat any longer, to him or Danny. He was dead. Hawk holstered his weapon and turned the stranger's hard, leathered face toward the firelight. There was nothing familiar about the man's countenance, his yellowed teeth clenched in the rictus of death. He left the dead man and walked into the shadows to find Danny, almost tripping over him where he lay hog-tied outside the circle of light.

"Hey! Watch it!"

Hawk bent over and cut him loose.

"Just saved your hide, young 'un. Guess if anybody has a right to stomp on it, it's me."

Danny laughed, climbing to his feet, rubbing his wrists, and rolling his shoulders to alleviate the discomfort of his partially healed body. "Can't argue that."

"Recognize him?"

"Naw. Hell, I figured him for one of the fellas you said were after you."

Hawk shrugged. "Don't know."

He quickly searched the dead man's pockets, coming up with only a few dollars, a pocket full of extra cartridges, and some papers stuffed into an inside pocket. He jerked the papers out, noticing they were unusually stiff, and unfolded them across his knee, smoothing them flat with a gunman's smooth hands. They were a packet of wanted fliers.

"Bounty hunter," Hawk stated flatly, his voice filled with disgust.

"A bounty hunter?"

His friend thrust the heavy, rough paper under his nose. The center of the page was filled with a line drawing of Danny, and, though it was unflattering, it was recognizable. At the bottom was a detailed description of both Danny and Hawk, Danny's name in large letters, and Hawk unnamed. The reward for Danny was an even thousand dollars, alive, with an extra five hundred bonus thrown in, if the lucky man who retrieved Danny also managed to come up with his partner, sitting in, or slung over, a saddle. Obviously this huckleberry had decided over the saddle was easier. The man offering the reward was one Ansel Miller of Miller, Texas. A man with the same name as the town he lived in was no doubt a man of considerable influence, one used to getting what he wanted. The stepfather who wanted his stepson hung.

"Knew Ansel was likely to do somethin' like this," Danny observed, "just didn't think he'd get around to it this fast."

"Guess you were wrong."

"When do we pull out?"

"Morning. I'll take care of him while you get the coffee and grub on."

"What if he had a friend?"

"Doesn't seem likely a bushwhacking bounty hunter would have many friends. My guess is he stumbled on you by pure accident. Even a blind pig will find an acorn every once in a while. I'll take first watch tonight."

"Sure thing."

They ate swiftly, washed it all down with steaming coffee,

then snuffed the fire to nothing when Danny sought his blankets to grab a few hours of much needed, healing sleep.

Hawk gazed uneasily across the rolling hills surrounding their camp. He was finding more and more that, if he closed his injured eye, the sight sharpened in the other. A blessing, considering where there was one bounty hunter, there would sooner or later be more. It was not a thought to calm a man's nerves. Hawk had seen his share of trouble. He knew that at a gut level, but now he had a price on his head. He understood there *might* be others attached to another life, but with ever more frequent flashes of insight grew the certainty that there were no others.

He listened to the sounds of the night. Birds softly cooed to one another in subdued voices. Coyotes howled and yapped in the distance as the moon rose above the far hills. Sounds of the night, uninterrupted, were a comfort to a man standing watch in the darkness. If something approached that did not belong, he would know it.

Chapter Eight

By the time they rode together into Stillwater, Hawk felt he was where he needed to be. Danny hung off his left out of habit, his hand resting on the rifle butt where it protruded above his knee, eyes scanning the street. The kid looked more fit than he had a right to be, but that gave Hawk some ease.

This was where his inexplicable drive had brought him — to this fair-size huddle of buildings, squatting on either side of a couple of dusty streets. Like train tracks, they ran parallel to the bordering mountains on one side and open desert on the other. Nothing looked familiar about the place, but Hawk was determined he was not leaving until he understood why he had had to come here. Why had his inner, driving urge to move west become abated now, giving him peace? Why did the name Ethan plague him?

"You gonna tell me what we're doin' here any time soon?" Danny asked, interrupting his thoughts.

"I plan on staying a spell."

" 'Twasn't what I asked."

Hawk cast Danny a sideways look. He knew what the boy was getting at, but he had no answers for him. At least none that made any sense yet.

Danny was another matter altogether, now. Hawk had grown genuinely fond of him since that day beneath the hangman's noose. He could only hope his liking for the kid would not end up getting the boy killed. Of course, they could split up. But each time he gave consideration to the possibility, he remembered the wanted posters on Danny's head and though the boy, a young gun if he had ever seen one, had learned caution and gained skills, he was still green, and alone — no matter his own opinion on the matter. Danny would be wolf meat in less time than the older man cared to think about.

Danny chuckled. "I swear, you are the slipperiest, most closed-mouthed, strangest man I ever met."

"Couldn't've met many others," Hawk countered with a grunt.

"If we're gonna light and set a spell, you're gonna have to give me some straight answers, like I give you. I reckon I owe you my skin, but I'd kinda like to know why I'm ridin' into some spit an' holler town where I just might get my head blowed off right along with yours."

It was true enough, Hawk had to admit to himself, as they crossed into the outside edge of the small town. Danny had made no bones about the fact that he had not even started out in this world legitimately. He had been raised never knowing who his real father had been — his mother, as pretty a thing as ever lived in his eyes, had married his stepfather to give him a roof over his head and an honorable name. But things had not gone as she had planned. Ansel Miller had turned out to be a cruel, greedy man who had beaten her when the mood struck and had taken a strap to the young Danny frequently for real or imagined offenses. It hadn't taken the kid long to learn it didn't much matter what he did, Ansel was bound to come after him sooner or later. So he had made plans to light out a short time before his mother died of the fever. Had been implementing them, in fact, when Hawk had run across him. At the moment, Hawk felt he knew more about his young companion than he did about himself, and that made for a very uneasy feeling in the pit of his stomach.

The horses continued to plod down the dusty stretch before them. A few people, scattered the length of the main street, threw curious glances in their direction, acknowledging the arrival of strangers.

"I don't have any answers for you, Danny."

"Don't have, or reckon you won't give?"

Hands loose on the saddle horn, reins dangling between fingers, Hawk gave the kid the truth. "I don't remember much of anything before some yahoo's bullet creased my skull, and I took a dive off the back of a paddle wheel river boat."

"Why'd they want to shoot you in the first place?"

"Don't know the answer to that, either. But let me tell you, it's sort of like having mice skittering around in the attic. A body knows they're there, but he rarely lays eyes on one. Lately things have been coming back. I just need something to sort of pull it all together, and I know that here is where I'm gonna find it."

Danny shook his head. "You don't know who's after you, or why, but you're ridin' into this town where you figure they do know, and you're gonna wait for someone to try to cave your skull in a second time so you can find out?"

"That's about it."

"You *are* plumb crazy." The boy laughed out loud, drawing new, questioning looks from a couple of nearby citizens. "But we're partners, and I'm stickin'. You think you'll find your answers here . . . maybe, you will. Even the biggest ball of twine unravels."

"Let's find us a place to cut the grit, then see about finding some work and a place to stay," Hawk suggested, drawing his horse up in front of the local saloon and stepping down from the saddle.

A tall, rangy man, tanned dark from constant exposure to

the sun, emerged from the saloon, gave Hawk a long, searching look, then turned and mounted his horse, riding out of town in a plume of dust.

Danny drew his rifle from the boot beside his knee and hopped down, all the while staring after the departing stranger.

"Know him?" Danny asked.

"Naw, not him. But I know the breed . . . first cousin to a rattlesnake, but I'm bettin' he knew me."

"*Sheeeit,*" Danny observed.

"Just don't let him get behind you, Danny boy," Hawk observed as they entered the saloon.

The place was empty — not an uncommon occurrence for the early afternoon in a town other than one where there was a gold or silver boom.

"Whiskey," Hawk ordered as the bartender, a broad-shouldered, bald-headed, jolly soul, approached them. "And bring my friend a beer," he added before Danny could open his mouth.

The kid grunted his acceptance and hooked his elbows on the edge of the bar, starting to feel the strain of a long day on the trail on a barely healed body.

The barkeep returned with a heavy stride, laying meaty forearms on the saloon bar in friendly camaraderie. "You boys passing through?"

Hawk shook his head. The best source of information in any town was its bartender. Hawk looked at this one and took the man's measure. Business was slow, and he was itching to talk.

"We're stayin' a spell," Hawk said amiably. "Hope to find a decent place to stay and some honest work."

"Stillwater's an open door to new folks who think like you." The bartender thrust out a thick, short hand. "Name's Jasper Lynch. Been here five years now. It's a good town. Got its problems, but it's still a good town. Solid. Lots of good things in the future, I can tell you. That's why I put down my roots."

"Don't look like much," Danny said uncharitably, then took a long pull on his warm beer.

"Don't have to," Jasper said with a sour twist of his lips. "Good people and a solid town. The combination ain't exactly as plentiful as ticks on a dog."

"Don't let the kid get your goat," Hawk interjected. "You say there're some good jobs to be had?"

"The pair of you look like you've got some sand. If'n you do, best place in town is the Burr Stage and Freight Line. They've been having some trouble lately, so they're paying fighting wages. Best place to stay is the boarding house right down the street. Miss Ella will make you feel right to home."

Hawk tossed back his whiskey, placing the thick, heavy glass on the polished bar with a hollow thump. "Obliged." He turned and headed for the door. Danny was hard pressed to follow without giving up the remains of his beer.

Rona watched them ride into town, the pair of strangers, one obviously a gunman, or close kin to one, and the other hardly more than a boy, half-curled fingers resting on the rifle butt beside his knee. She frowned, and it was more than sunlight causing it. The pair of strangers appeared trail weary and travel hardened — like hell with the hide peeled off.

"Ty, Jake, come on out here," she called softly over her shoulder into the Burr Line office. She nodded toward the pair as they dismounted in front of the saloon.

"What do you make of that?"

"Trouble," Tyler said quickly.

"Good man to have on yer side." Jake chewed and spat.

"You figure to offer 'em a job? If'n you don't, I'll figure *you* for plumb loco."

"You can think whatever you want, you old coot." Rona leaned against the hitching rail. "They haven't asked for work yet."

"Who sez you have to wait fer 'em to ask?"

"They'll probably try to hold me up for wages if I go to them," Rona responded. "God knows what Jasper's telling those two."

"Neither one looks like driver material to me," Tyler put in.

"An' *you* do, I s'pose," Jake nearly snarled. "You weren't much yerself when Rona's pa took you in, an' I'll never understand why Hank kept you on."

Tyler's black eyes glinted. A feline smile curved his lips but did not go any further than that. "Shut up, old man," his tone was bantering, but his words were sharp-edged.

"Neither one of you has anything intelligent to say," Rona responded irritably. "If we're going to start fighting each other, I might as well shut down the line."

She turned and walked back into the office without looking back.

Jake followed in a heartbeat, casting Tyler a measuring look that should have cut the man off at the knees, but, instead, he brought up the rear, closing the door behind them once they were inside.

Rona moved to the window, glancing once more out onto the street as the two strangers came out of the saloon. She spoke to Jake over her shoulder.

"How do I know they aren't something Sam Reo sent for?"

The old man chuckled. "Looks more like somethin' Hank would've sent for."

Rona gave an indignant snort. "Hank would never. . . ."

"Told you he did hisself. Mebbe they're them."

"If they are, they'll find me soon enough. Besides, Hank wasn't the kind of man who would know a pair like that."

"Like what?" Tyler interjected. "Don't look like much to me. A pair of drifters, one of 'em mighty green. Might be able to handle a team, if you plan on hirin' a couple new drivers."

Jake gaffawed. "You're a mite dense, son. Don't have to look at that older fella twice to know he'd win most powder-burnin' contests. You'll never find that young 'un sittin' on his gun hand, neither."

"They don't matter. The one I'm keeping an eye on is right out there." Rona nodded toward the general store across the street where Sam Reo was just emerging.

"You got the right instinct, Miss Rona," Tyler said seriously.

"Wish to Jasper she did," Jake muttered to himself, shaking his head and turning away from the pair at the window.

Outside, Reo slung a flour sack of supplies over his saddle horn, swung astride an exceptional bay gelding, and started him out down the street at a light-footed trot. He glanced in Rona's direction, catching sight of her through the window, touched the brim of his hat politely, and nodded a greeting.

Her frown deepened.

On his horse, headed out of town, Sam Reo contemplated Rona Burr. She was a pretty thing, truth be told, but tough as leather, and a more stubborn, determined woman he'd never run across. When he caught sight of her in the window of the Burr Line offices, Tyler Harding was standing close beside her. Whatever the tie was between those two, Sam didn't like it.

Chapter Nine

Later, after they had checked into the boarding house, and each had taken a bath to soak out the trail dust, Hawk and Danny strolled up to the bulletin board in front of the Burr Line office. The bartender had steered them true. The outfit was hiring shotgun riders as well as drivers.

"Reckon these folks got a little too much time on their hands?" Danny queried of Hawk as they both became very much aware that almost every eye in town was on them.

"Town's got more trouble than the friendly barkeep wanted to let on," Hawk observed.

"Somethin' we want to steer clear of."

"Most of the time, yes."

"*Most* of the time?"

Hawk felt uncomfortable. It was like a bubble about to burst. There was something tugging at the back door of his memory . . . and it was very near.

"I'm signing on with the stageline."

"Are you loco? Looks like a sucker job. They must be losin' men on every run to be payin' those kinda wages."

"It's where I need to be, Danny. I'm not asking you to come along for the ride. Could be the livery or saloon is hiring."

Danny laughed out loud. "You're kiddin' me, right? We're partners, an' I can handle a full team as well as any man. Won't find nobody better to ride shotgun, neither."

Hawk chuckled. "We ain't hired yet."

"Hell, with a notice like that, they'd hire anythin' that kin walk an' handle a team."

"You're probably right."

"Damn' right I'm right! Sure you don't want to give this some extra thought?"

Raw words spoken in a superior sneer broke into their conversation. "Kid's got a good idea. Stillwater ain't healthy. Especially workin' for the Burr outfit."

A lean, dark stranger stepped up on the boardwalk from the dusty street, flicking dirt from beneath his fingernails with an Arkansas toothpick. He wore his gun low, giving Hawk cause to figure him to belong to the same snake family as the fellow they'd crossed paths with earlier.

"Don't see that it's any of your affair, what we do," Hawk said carefully.

The stone-faced stranger put his knife away with slow, definite movements, leaving his gun hand free. Obvious was the fact he was intent on discouraging them from signing on with the freight and stage line. What wasn't quite so clear was how far the man was prepared to go to accomplish that.

"We're lookin' for honest work," Danny interposed.

"This sure ain't the place to find it. I'm just tryin' to be helpful." The stranger's voice took on a faint whine. He cocked his head, holding them within his sight, oddly pinning them from the corners of his eyes. "You know this place is jinxed? Yeah. They have more bad luck'n any outfit I ever did see." He couldn't quite smother the grin. "Why, they're havin' accidents, losing stock, getting themselves robbed, and" — he said it pointedly — "gettin' their drivers killed on a regular basis. Jest comin' close to this place is enough to make a man fall on hard times."

There it was. The words were barely spoken, the threat a

cold ripple on the air, when Hawk heard the distinctive double click of Danny's rifle being cocked. The kid might not know beans about a six-gun, but he could bring that rifle of his into play faster than most men could draw a hand gun. He had seen him do it often, practicing or going after rabbits for their dinner. The question now was . . . could he use it on something other than rabbits? It was a question Hawk wished he had had answered before now, but there was no help for it. Now was the time.

"You got more to say, you best get it said. We've got business." Hawk took a step toward the cold-eyed stranger, crowding him.

It was a direct move, one calculated to back up the granite-faced man, and it worked. A cold chill raced up Hawk's spine. Danny was on his right, leaving his blind side open to the street. For only a moment they had let their guard down, and it was the moment that counted. He found the clammy sweat of fear an unwelcome visitor. An instant later there came the soft tapping. The kid, beating a rhythmic tattoo on the wooden stock of his rifle.

There was someone off to Hawk's left, sidling up on his blind side. Danny had told him on the trail, over his protests, that he would do something to warn him in a situation such as this. The air suddenly thickened. It was pure tension, a circumstance with which he felt himself to be familiar. He knew this kind of thing had happened to him before. Like bits of rancid meat, pieces of his past life were not to be ignored. His face remained impassive. The glint of steel in his blue eyes flashed a deadly warning — one that, for those who had known Ethan Torregrossa before, would rip into their guts with knife-edged fear.

It was clear the man facing him had no real intention of taking him alone in a stand-up gunfight. His eyes betrayed him. Hawk's gut told him few men could take him. That assurance electrified the air.

The clicking from Danny's fingers grew more insistent. Hawk did not shift his eyes. He knew where the second man was now, he could feel him, sense his presence across the street. The arrogant stranger should have chosen his partner better.

Hawk was already rotating when the fool on his blind side turned the confrontation into a powder-burning contest. A couple of man-size splinters peeled up at their feet on the boardwalk with the ear-splitting crack of a six-gun. Danny's rifle exploded nearly simultaneously, sending the other man somersaulting out of a second-story window across the street as the arrogant stranger pulled blue lightning. The kid's rifle had coughed an instant before Hawk's six-gun, nailing a target Hawk hadn't seen clearly.

That damn' kid saved my hide, Hawk thought as his six-gun bucked in his hand and the arrogant stranger went down, writhing in the street, clutching at his bleeding thigh. Then Hawk dropped to one knee, bringing his still smoking pistol to bear on yet another man, well armed, stepping out of the stage office.

Danny was still moving. His rifle swung around, centering somewhere on the newcomer's belt buckle, and his young face was set and hard, brown eyes glittering with the brutal excitement of the moment. Trial by fire. The kid had proved he could handle more than rabbits.

Tyler Harding froze, rifle in hand, pointing the barrel harmlessly toward the sky.

"Just stepped out to lend a hand." He ground out the words. "But it looks like you don't need it."

Hawk and Danny eased off a bit, but kept their weapons pointed in his general direction.

"Gentlemen," Tyler now said blandly, his voice losing its edge as everyone appeared to relax, "welcome to Stillwater. Step on inside. Miss Rona would like to meet you. If you're looking for work, you've come to the right place."

A sheriff, tall and bulky, appeared out of nowhere with the proper mixture of annoyance and concern etched across his fleshy face. He stopped first alongside the man who had spilled out of the second-story window and showed no signs of further movement, then gave his attention to the man who had started it all. The man was lying in the dusty street, writhing in pain. The sheriff ordered a couple of Stillwater's citizens to haul the wounded man off to the doctor, and then the somewhat rotund lawman came on over to the men standing in front of the stage office.

"What the hell's goin' on here, Harding?" the lawman demanded.

Tyler shrugged, lowering the rifle he had not used. "You'll have to ask these gentlemen, Sheriff Samovic. I came in a little late."

"Self-defense, Sheriff," Hawk answered for them both. "They tried to gun us."

"Now, why would they have call to try an' do that? You're strangers in town. You ain't even seed each other before . . . have you?"

Danny took an instant dislike to the lawman, bristling silently under his scrutiny. Still, he lowered his rifle, but kept his finger curled around the trigger.

Samovic continued staring at Danny. He took the kid's measure in an eye blink. A youngster with a rifle who could take a man out of a second-story window across a street with the sun against him bore watching, and the sheriff was beginning to think his jail would be the best place to keep an eye on him.

"Well," he began, "till we get to the truth of this, I think you boys better hand over your guns and. . . ."

"And what?" Rona Burr asked, appearing at the doorway of the stage office. "You've already gotten the truth of it. They told you. It was self-defense. I saw it all from the window. So did Tyler and Jake." She shot Ty an angry look. "Tyler just doesn't appear to want to talk much about it. I asked him to go out into it. Didn't seem wise to have two men gunned down on my front steps with everything else that's been going on around here lately. Especially seeing as how they're my new driver and shotgun."

"Hell's bells, Rona, why didn't you say so?"

"I just did." She turned to Hawk and Danny. "Come on inside, and I'll give you the welcome speech."

She hovered off-center in the open doorway, dressed in pants and loose-fitting homespun shirt, not even pretending to spare any further attention to the sheriff and his troubles.

The lawman stomped off, and the crowd in the street started to break up as Rona led the way into the shady coolness of the stage office.

"You boys looking for work?" she asked before they were entirely through the door, Ty trailing along behind, not completely turning his back on the street until the heavy, wooden door was closed behind them.

Rona strolled over to the stove where a coffee pot was steaming. She took a couple of tin cups from hooks above it and sloshed some of the strong, black brew into each before handing one to Hawk and then one to Danny.

"Have a seat," she gestured toward the rough table and surrounding chairs on the far side of the room.

"Howdy, young fellas!" Jake said as he entered at a casual amble from the back door. He laid aside an ancient-looking shotgun with an aplomb that made Hawk wonder what the

76

old fellow had been doing out back during all the excitement.

"Guess you two are a-huntin' work. Well, this here's the best place to work I ever lit at. Miss Rona's a boss to ride the river with."

"We could use jobs," Hawk admitted, tasting the dark liquid in his cup and finding it strong and bitter, just to his liking. "But it appears like lookin' for work is a dangerous business in this town."

Rona smiled, and that made all the difference in the world. Her face, round and youthful, but lined with sadness, took on an angelic radiance. Hazel eyes lit up, and right then and there Hawk knew he would like to see them filled with mischief. He was willing to bet there were times when they had been in the past.

"Kinda looks like that, doesn't it?" Rona said. "But it depends on who you tell you're looking for work, and where you go to find it. The sign outside says we pay fighting wages." She poured herself a half cup of the bitter coffee and sat down with them. "The reason is simple. Sooner or later, if you're working for me, you're going to be put in a position where you're going to have to fight. You've already had a sample."

Danny grinned. "Looks like we're working for you, then," he piped up, waving his cup with a flourish. "Hell, if we're gonna get ourselves shot at, we might as well get paid proper wages."

Hawk couldn't agree more, but there was something in addition to that. Something here that caused him to be more interested in Rona Burr than he should be. Within him something stirred. Something rose to the top and hovered there, ready to burst like a boil. He shifted uneasily in his chair, the wood creaking its protest in a noisy groan that echoed across the room.

"Well," Rona said, sipping her coffee and looking straight at Hawk, "we still need a stage driver and a man to ride shotgun."

"I'll do the drivin'," Danny volunteered, and nodded toward Hawk, "if'n he'll do the shootin'."

"You've got yourself a gun guard," Hawk agreed, "but it comes with a string attached. I want the story behind your trouble. I want to know what we're going to be facing out there."

Rona shrugged. "Why not? You can walk into either saloon in town and hear the whole story anyway. It might as well be from me."

"I don't know, Rona," Tyler put in.

"Shet up. She's doin' the right thing," Jake countermanded him, eyeing Hawk closely, appraisingly.

"It doesn't matter if I am or not," Rona said evenly. "I need the driver and shotgun. I'm that desperate. It was already started when my father died, but then it just got that much worse. Tyler had been here a short time, working for my pa. Sam Reo had just arrived in town. My brother, Hank, and I decided to keep the business going, and we would've managed all right if we had been left alone. But, all of a sudden strange things started happening. Little things at first, like finding the spokes in one of the wheels broken. Hank had to spend all morning fixing it, and it made the stage late for its run. Some freight deliveries got mixed up and some stolen. Then, one of our drivers was nearly beaten to death in a saloon brawl. We weren't sure about that at first, but then it started happening more often. Men working for the Burr Line had to be armed and in pairs to be safe until even that wasn't enough, and they started quitting."

Hawk looked at her intently, waiting for the rest. He sloshed the coffee, looked into the cup, then back at her. His calm façade hid the turmoil within. His gut was churning with the certainty that he was close to what he sought. So very close.

"They ain't gonna run us off," Danny said cockily.

"Good for you, young 'un!" Jake encouraged him.

Hawk barely heard them. His attention was centered on the woman, on the words flowing from her lips, and the stubborn lift of her small chin.

"Hank was certain Sam Reo was behind all the trouble, but he couldn't prove it. He didn't know why, since Reo arrived in Stillwater, blowing smoke about how he wanted to help the town grow, to make it a place for families, and to convince the railroad to come in. He started looking at some land around town, always hinting he was there to buy. Things kept happening to us. Accidents, more injures, and there didn't seem to be anything we could do. Hank was no gunman, but Sam Reo is. People can see that six-gun of his. My brother decided to call in a few chips. He sent a letter to a man, one who put his gun up for hire, along with a couple of hundred dollars and travel expenses. He told me he had done the man a favor, that there was honor among such men, and he wouldn't let him down. Hank was dead a week after he posted that letter, killed in a freight wagon crash that was no accident. That was over four months ago, and that gunman he wrote to in New Orleans is probably laughing himself sick over anyone who would be dumb enough to send all that money across the country with no guarantee it wouldn't be stolen outright."

The bubble burst. All that Hawk was came flooding back, filling in the empty spots in a swamping wave. He shuddered. He had no idea how his face must look to Rona who continued talking quietly in the background, unaware of his sudden inner revelation. Danny gave him a peculiar look, wondering what was wrong. Hawk finally understood what had been driving him to this destination. He had come because he had to, because he had been paid to do a job. He had been ambushed on the river boat. But still he had kept coming on, straining to fulfill his obligation to Hank Burr. He *was* the Hawk, a peculiar hybrid of gunman and lawman. One who had and could end a range war almost single-handedly, turning the victory to the highest bidder. A man able to clean up a rough town . . . for a price. He lived high when the money flowed, but was equally capable of living off the land when the well ran dry. The memories flowed while his eyes remained fastened on Rona. He inhaled deeply, flicking his glance toward Jake who was staring openly at him, a measuring look in his eye. There was just one more thing.

"Did your brother name this fellow?"

"Ethan Torregrossa."

Danny stared at his companion, enthralled by the transformation of the man's eyes, flat and dead in appearance, taking on an icy glint at the sound of that name.

Ethan stilled, the last piece of the puzzle in place, then nodded. "Guess we're in. When do we roll?"

Rona looked relieved. "Tomorrow morning. At first light."

Ethan rose from his chair, Danny scrambling to keep pace, and started for the door.

"Wait a minute!" Rona laughed. "I didn't even get your names."

"Danny," the kid volunteered more quickly than he should have, considering the wanted fliers. At least he had the sense not to spit out his last name.

"Folks call me Hawk," Ethan said over his shoulder. "We'll be back at first light."

They left the stage offices and headed down the street toward the boarding house.

"What happened back there? You know this Torregrossa,

don't you?" Danny blurted out the instant they were safely clear of Miss Burr and her cronies. Nice enough folks, but still little more than strangers. "You gonna tell me what you know about him?"

"You're talking to him," Ethan answered quietly. He met the kid's startled gaze directly, then they walked on.

Chapter Ten

Rona crossed her arms over her chest and stood by the window, eyes following Hawk and his much younger companion. *Hawk* . . . she mulled the name over in her mind. From the moment she had laid eyes on him, she had liked him, and that was putting aside the fact that he had shot down a man whom she was sure was in the employ of Sam Reo. She felt strength emanating from him, but there was a dark side as well, a dangerous side. She toyed with the idea that this might be the breed of man Hank would have sent for.

The presence of the boy puzzled her. He was young, but obviously aging rapidly under the more experienced man's tutelage. Hawk, as he called himself, had probably lived beyond his years. For better or worse, however, Danny had hitched his wagon to the older man's star, and they were now partners. Yet, they might be the best damned thing that ever happened to Burr Stage and Freight Line.

"Well I'll be an egg-sucking coyote!" Danny couldn't help grinning. "You remembered something."

"I remembered pretty much everything."

"Torregrossa," Danny murmured with some awe to his voice, shaking his head.

"I'll expect you to keep this to yourself until I tell you differently."

"You should've just told her."

"Why?"

"She figures her brother for a sucker. Reckons he tried to do something or another, but then just up and died on her before anything happened. He didn't, though. He sent for you."

"She also didn't think it was such a good idea, if you remember." Hawk shrugged. "Maybe she's right. But that doesn't matter much. What matters is I want the say in this. And I say it's better for her to go on thinking I'm just a shotgun rider on her stage, until I can get the lay of the land. She believes what she's sayin', but it seems to me there's more buried here than what's on the surface."

"You figure there's more trouble here than just this Sam Reo, or you figure maybe he ain't it?"

"Can't rightly say . . . now . . . but it looks like I'm gonna find out. If you're riding with me on this thing, you better learn right off that you don't trust anyone, don't turn your back on anyone . . . and I mean *anyone* . . . without me covering you. I've been in a situation like this a time or two, and most times the men involved in this kind of a fight are natural born back-shooters. Remember that, and maybe you'll stay alive."

"I'm riding with you," Danny replied firmly. "We're partners, just like we said."

"All right, partner, let's get to our room and catch some rest. First light comes mighty early, and whoever's behind the trouble in this town isn't going to like us dealing ourselves in."

Swinging his rifle up, resting the barrel over his shoulder, the kid chuckled softly. "Reckon they already declared war back there in front of the stage office."

"That wasn't war, Danny, that was just the opening skirmish. I have a feeling we're gonna know we were in a helluva fight before this is over."

A shiver ran up Ethan's spine. Everything was once again in place. Memories were whole — some more clearly than he liked.

Dawn was streaking the eastern horizon orange and gray, when Torregrossa and Danny showed up behind the stage office where Rona was already engaged in harnessing up the team. The old man, Jake, appeared around the corner, carrying more gear, and split a grin fit to bust a gut when he clapped eyes on the new arrivals.

"Knew you'd show."

"We hired on," Ethan stated quietly.

Jake bobbed his head. "Sure did, but there was some others did the same an' never showed."

Danny lent a hand to settling harnesses and tightening down buckles while his companion gave Jake a hand, tossing first the gear up top, then some small freight.

"Carson City run," Rona said with authority. "I'm expecting you boys to be pulling out in no more than fifteen minutes. We have a couple of paying passengers waiting inside, a few small packages for Carson City, and some mail riding up top under the seat." The sun was a gleaming sliver in the east. "We're not a very big operation, not much more than a thread connecting us with Carson City, but we're hanging on, and I expect you to get this stage, and everything on it, through in one piece. I have plans to extend this line to Placerville in California and even on to Sacramento. Don't let me down."

"We'll do what we hired on to do." Ethan was brusque.

"He does the talkin' for us both," Danny said.

Ty Harding strolled out in the gray dawn light, glancing at the rig as Danny swung up, starting the stage swaying on its over-size springs before he settled in and collected the reins in his hands. He was amazed the woman had hung on this long and wondered how much longer she could do it. How soon would the Burr Line disappear after being his shield for so long? And, did he have enough time to risk easing off a bit in order to set the business up for a hit worthy of his plans before leaving Reo blinded in the dust when he disappeared?

Harding looked around for his men and spotted one down the length of the alley across the main street, lounging against a post. He was going to have to be careful. He still wasn't certain about how much Reo knew.

"I don't know, Rona, it might be better if you postponed this run," Tyler muttered to the Burr Line's mistress as she stepped back from the team, and Hawk climbed up beside Danny. "This pair is about as green as they come. I know how desperate you are to keep things goin', but you might be taking a big risk with your passengers."

Rona laughed out loud, casting Ty an amused look. "That pair might be a lot of things I haven't even thought of yet, but green they're not."

"Eh? Green he says!" Jake snapped, glowering at the younger man. "That Hawk is tough as old boot leather and savvy as an Injun. You'd have to be wet behind the ears yourself to be thinkin' of that pair as green."

"Kid's green as grass," Ty insisted.

"It doesn't matter," Rona interrupted them. "I have a feeling they're gonna stick. Now come on, we have to get that stage out on time, and then we have a freight shipment to get ready to roll."

Ty took another look in his man's direction and spotted Reo, riding into town.

"Ty, help the passengers with their baggage, please," Rona

called to him as they went in through the back door. "Everything else is set. This stage is ready to roll out on time for a change."

Danny drew the stage to a halt in front of the stage office, sitting with reins loosely held between his fingers as a couple of passengers emerged from the building and climbed on board.

"At least there ain't no ladies on this run," Danny said softly when he saw Ethan taking note of their passengers.

Torregrossa nodded and swung his attention in a new direction as Rona emerged from the office and froze in her tracks, eyes fixed on the lone rider making his way up the street.

"Has to be Reo," he remarked to Danny, inclining his head toward the rust-haired rider they had seen the previous day.

Sam Reo in the early light was an even more imposing figure of a man, heavily built, square-featured, and dark-skinned. That thick crop of rust-colored straw, trapped beneath his hat, extended into thick sideburns reaching all the way to his jawline. And the eyes. Ethan recognized the type of eyes. They were slate gray, flat, and penetrating. The eyes of a cold man, a man with few, if any, feelings that might get in the way of a job. There was a stillness about Reo, a look about him, a feeling with which Ethan was not unfamiliar.

Reo smiled, or at least curved his lips, and touched his hat brim to Rona with a gentlemanly nod of his head as he rode past at a leisurely pace. Rona turned abruptly away, handing a spare shotgun up to Ethan who had Danny's rifle leaning against a thigh.

"You ride tight and watch yourselves," Rona said to them both, keeping her voice low. "I've got a lot riding on this trip, and I don't want your hides on my conscience, too."

Ethan nodded in the direction of Reo's receding form. "That Sam Reo?"

Rona nodded.

"You said he was after the Burr Line. A man like that doesn't usually mess with something as small as your outfit. You got any idea why he'd do such a thing? Did your brother do something to get crossways of him maybe?"

"Of course not, Hank was a good man!"

"Good men make enemies."

Rona snorted.

Torregrossa was intrigued by her tightly compressed lips and the stubborn look on her face, but he didn't have time to think about it before Tyler tossed a couple of heavy bags into the rear boot of the stage, and Rona hurried back inside. Ethan caught a glimpse of Ty Harding's face as he, in turn, stared after Sam Reo. Ty Harding had thrown Reo a malignant glare which, despite the situation, set the new gun guard's teeth on edge. Harding was another man Ethan decided to keep an eye on. And he was going to have to do it discreetly, since Rona obviously trusted the man.

Damn, he wished he wasn't leaving town for a couple of days so soon after arriving — after remembering. But he had no choice. He and the kid had signed on and to do anything else now would be too hard to explain. Besides, the stage was the main target, and, if there was trouble, he would be on it. No harm had come to Rona in Stillwater since her brother's death when he had not been there. But trouble followed the stage like a plague. Ethan, without reservation, hoped it would follow it again. He and the kid could handle whatever got thrown at them.

The passengers settled themselves inside when Sam Reo, having dismounted, appeared again, emerging from the general store that had opened early enough to accommodate his needs.

Reo's hard, flat eyes now clapped themselves onto Harding who was just dragging another couple of bags out of the office, tossing them into the back of the stage with the others. The black hatred in that stare seemed an acknowledgment of the hunted meeting the hunter. To Ethan their appraising looks at each other reminded him of a pair of cocks exchanging looks before fighting to the death. The question was, which was which? A thin, cruel smile curled the corners of Reo's lips in a fleeting promise Ethan had good cause to wonder about, and then the man remounted, turning his horse back the way he'd come.

Rona reappeared at that moment, and Reo, spotting her, once again touched his hat brim to her in a gentlemanly fashion before he lifted his mount to a gallop, heading out of town. Rona froze where she was, staring after him, as dust rose in his wake. Her fair features, whipped into a high blush by her early morning labors, stilled to a bitter mask. Her bright eyes flashed fire, and her chin was thrust out. Ethan sympathized. For Rona to be able to do anything about the man called Reo, she had to have proof. The law would need to have proof.

Ethan Torregrossa needed only his gun.

Chapter Eleven

Rona watched the stage pull out with a lurch, knowing the risks anyone was taking who rolled with a Burr Line stage. Her gut told her that the men driving it this time were different, but she wasn't sure if that made things better or worse. The chances of the stage getting through unstopped were not good, and their unbending determination raised the odds on their getting themselves killed. While she did not want to lose the stage and freight line, neither did she relish the idea of more men dying for it.

She glanced at Tyler where he stood, also watching the stage depart. He wore an odd expression on his face. Without a second thought she categorized it as worry, and turned to go back inside the office, but she hesitated in the doorway, watching as the stage grew smaller in the distance.

Through all the trials since her father's death, and then that of her brother's, Ty had sided with her. He had hired on with her father. That had been recommendation enough for her to keep him on as things continued to go badly. He had driven freight wagons alone or in tandem with Hank or herself. He did whatever was needed, doing it without complaint. He had been a big help, despite Jake's reservations.

Still, when that pair had showed up yesterday, looking for work, Rona had regarded the event as a sign things would soon be improving. Jake had a way of sometimes rattling on, but he was right about the two new hands and the experience the older one had under his belt. Now, though, as she stood watching the stage disappear into the distance, she was not so sure she had been right. A twinge of foreboding swept over her. A shiver that brought back the memory of the day her brother had taken out the freight wagon for the last time.

She grasped the doorknob, turned it, and stepped inside, half expecting Ty to follow her. When he didn't, she gave a puzzled frown, but let it go when Jake pounded in through the back door with his usual scraping and thumping of boots.

"Freight wagon's ready to roll," the old-timer announced. Then he caught her expression and grunted. "You got to get your mind off that Reo fella. Tunnel vision don't help nobody."

"He killed Hank."

"You got no proof. Nothin' but Hank's own scattered ideas on the subject, an' that was afore the accident."

"Well, since he showed up in Stillwater, men have started dying. What other kind of a reading would you put on that?"

"There were others showed up around the same time. Tyler Harding fer one."

Rona put her hands on her hips. "What do you have against him, Jake? He does his job. What more can he do?"

Jake shrugged. "That ain't the question, an' you don't rightly want to hear my answers. Just be careful . . . real careful . . . and, when you want to talk sensible about all this, you come an' see me. Right now, I got other work needs doin'."

"Just hold on a minute. You can't say something like that and then walk away. What's the matter with you and this town, anyway? What is it about Sam Reo that everybody likes so much they're willing to defend his every action?"

"Does it ever occur to you, girlie, that folks don't particularly *like* him? They just don't see him like you do."

"I see him very clearly."

"I don't think you do. You had your mind made up about him a long time ago, an' you don't want to hear nothin' else."

"He tried to buy the line right after Pa died!"

Jake shrugged. "Good businessman."

"Hank made it plain we weren't going to sell."

"Persistent son."

Rona strode over to her desk, dropping into the chair behind it with a loud creak of leather and wood. "Why do you care so much what I think of Sam Reo, Jake?"

"Hell, I don't give a fig about that. I just don't want you havin' your eyes closed to the truth when it rolls up on you."

"Sam Reo's a gunman. Everyone who cares to look can see it."

"So's Hawk."

"That's different."

"How?"

She flipped open the ledger in front of her and picked up a pen, tip poised above an inkwell.

"How?" Jake repeated the question, but didn't give her a chance to answer. "I'll tell you how," he said with a gravelly rasp. "You see Hawk different 'cause he's on your side. He's cut from the same cloth as Sam Reo."

Rona withheld the pen from the smooth black surface of the ink. "Jake, you've been a friend, but I'm not following you. Who exactly am I supposed to trust?"

"Yourself. Your gut an' your heart. It's what your daddy would've told you."

Rona fell silent, but it wasn't her daddy she was thinking about now, it was her mother. That woman would have taken one look at the cloak of omnipotence Sam Reo managed to wrap himself in and have declared the man the devil himself.

91

Just the look of the man would have been enough. Now, add his uncanny ability to know what the plans were to protect a shipment or the passengers, and the good woman would have been sent over the edge. What was puzzling was the influence he seemed to have on most of the people around him, including Jake.

She did trust herself to make judgments — or, at least, she had trusted herself in the past. Yet, now she hesitated in her thinking. There Jake was right. She had become dilatory. Since so many things had gone wrong, she had begun to question her own evaluations at every turn. She didn't discuss this with anyone, but she felt in her heart it was true. God knew she had been doing it again as the stage had pulled out.

"Got you thinkin', do I?" Jake grinned, tobacco-stained teeth showing unevenly behind the browned mustache. He hitched his rolling gait toward the back door. "Good," he said with a nod of his head, "I'll leave you to it."

Jake went out the back, allowing the door to bang shut behind him, and Rona was alone. Very much so. The silence of the room was oppressive as she glanced out the window, observing the activity on the street. It looked no different to her now than when her father and brother had been alive. She half expected to see one or the other of them walk around a corner and head for the door. Something should be different about it, damn it! It shouldn't look so infuriatingly, heart-wrenchingly the same. People she'd known for years greeting each other on the street. Dust rising in great gouts from beneath horses' hoofs or wagon wheels.

She allowed her thoughts to wander and could not help wondering, just for an instant, *what if Jake were right? Not excusing Reo's behavior or dismissing him as a candidate for being a murderer, but, if he had not been the one, then someone else had. Her brother had known he had been murdered as he lay dying.*

A strangling sigh forced its way from her constricted throat, and she jabbed the pen nib into the inkwell before her. She began to make entries, but her normally neat script was erratic, and the ink was leaving a chain of droplets in the scratches the pen made on the paper. *Damn it!* She jabbed the pen in the paper, in a moment draining the black ink into a large blotch. She couldn't be wrong in her judgment of Reo.

"If Sam Reo isn't the devil himself," Rona snapped bitterly, "then he is the closest thing to him I've ever come across."

Chapter Twelve

The horses moved easily beneath the traces as Danny guided them with firm, expert hands around the worst of the potholes and rocks that littered the old stage road. They were a couple of hours out of Stillwater, and everything was quiet, but a good stretch still lay before them.

"We're kickin' up dust," Danny said with good humor. "We'll be pullin' in on time with no problem."

"Maybe," Ethan allowed, "but don't go getting too cocky. Till we reach Carson City, trouble could be just around the next bend."

With that barely said, he pulled the canteen from beneath their swaying perch, jerked the cork, and tipped his head back for a deep draught. A bright flash from a ridge off to their left caught his good eye. Ethan lowered the canteen and focused in that direction, squinting against the brilliant sunlight.

Noting Ethan's alert, sudden silence, Danny flicked a quick glance in the direction he was looking. "Reo, damn his hide!"

"That's him, all right."

Ethan re-corked the canteen and stashed it beneath his seat, retrieving the shotgun in the same motion. With a quick look, he checked the loads, then propped the burnished wooden stock against his thigh, twin barrels pointing toward the sky. Reo, astride his bay gelding, could not miss the action.

Torregrossa meant it not as threat or challenge, but as a warning.

Sam Reo, sitting the ridge top, easy in the saddle, watched the Burr Line stage pass below him. He noted Hawk's action with some interest. He patted the pocket where the telegram he'd picked up in town lay folded against his chest. Now he had his assurance. Now he would move.

He looked down at Danny, handling those lines like an expert, and a cold wash of memory flooded over him. Danny looked like somebody's kid brother, and that was what had brought Sam Reo here — his kid brother. Clay Reo, Sam's younger brother by eight years, had been on the way to being somebody, to accomplishing something with his life. Sam had never thought of himself as counting for much. He lived precariously, taking on what jobs he could to fill his stomach, and then moving on. He had been a hard man, one pretty much battered by what he'd seen and done in life, when his brother hadn't been more than a sprout. But, from the beginning, he had seen something special in Clay. The boy had had a love of life and a determination to be somebody, working his way up in a bank, learning all he could, and finally opening his own banking establishment. And damned if people didn't trust Clay with their money! He'd been planning on getting married, too, to a pretty little thing with a lilt in her voice and blue eyes that could send a man reeling with one glance.

He remembered it all with a shudder that made his limbs tremble and his hands clench. Because the last time he had seen his kid brother, Clay had been hardly a man at all. He had been cut down during a bank robbery, shot twice in the back. It had been almost two months after it happened before Sam had gotten the news and made his way back to the kid's side. What he had found had chilled him to his soul. Clay had been braced in a chair with wheels, legs useless, one arm lifeless, the luster gone from his eyes, able to speak only in croaking, halting words. Sam had barely been able to stay in the same room with his own brother until after the shock had worn off. Then a fury such as he had never known had welled up within him with tidal force, and what little pity or empathy he had for the human race curled up inside him like a winter-frosted leaf. From that day forward his obsession had been finding the man who had maimed his brother, but he had failed, so far, in his quest. He had taken the money his brother had insisted he invest for them in the future since he was now unable to work. Sam had settled in Stillwater seven months back because he had heard whispers there were plans to bring in a railroad line. But all the while he had been keeping his ears open for any leads on the bank robbers who had shot his brother.

He gave the rocking stage one more look before turning his big bay from the edge of the ridge and heading back down. Lately, while he bided his time in Stillwater, trying to fit in with the local citizenry, the desire for vengeance had been getting stronger. It was a sweet, though phantom, taste that lay upon his tongue. He had only to locate and isolate his quarry. Whatever the risks, it didn't matter. Whoever or whatever stood in his way would be swept aside. The cold stone his heart had become held no room for pity, and his thirst for revenge frayed his patience, except for one spot of concern he felt for Rona Burr and her troubles. That concern was why he watched the stage whenever he had the opportunity, trying to find out who was behind the disasters the line kept encountering.

He turned his horse, sending him off at a lope down the steep incline. He had to plan, but more importantly he felt the need to move, to outrun the soul-eating hatred that was enveloping him.

Again Danny's eyes moved to the ridge above them and just in time to see the lone rider turn and disappear from view. Ethan's gaze remained fixed on the faint dust haze hanging on the cluster of rocks where Sam Reo had been.

"Reckon there'll be trouble?" The kid was antsy, anticipating the worst and bound to get it.

"Right there's your answer," Ethan grunted, and gave a sharp nod toward the road before them, only seconds before empty. Now three man spanned it, neckerchiefs across the lower halves of their faces, hats pulled low, and clothes the same dull, dusty browns. "That's no welcoming committee."

"Now what?" Danny's voice was tight, but he kept the horses moving.

"Now," Ethan answered eloquently, "we tear down their meathouse."

Some of the color left the boy's face, but a slow grin lifted the corners of his mouth as he tightened his grip on the reins and braced himself for the drive.

Torregrossa leaned over the side of the coach so he could talk to the two men within. "Trouble," he informed them bluntly. "If either of you gentlemen is carrying a gun, I suggest you get it out now."

The more well-dressed of the pair stuck his head out of the window, swaying with the rhythm of the coach and took himself a good look ahead at where the three outlaws blocked the road. A moment later a .45 filled his hand. He gave Ethan a business-like salute with the silvery barrel and disappeared back inside.

Thoroughly experienced along these lines, Ethan snapped

out an order to Danny on his left. "Get down in the boot. If they pick you off, we're done for."

"A coward'd hide in the boot," Danny resisted.

"Only a fool would stay up here and make a target out of himself when there was something he could do about it."

Danny slid down into the empty baggage boot at his feet, for the first time taking serious note of the fact that no baggage had been stashed there. It was all in the rear boot. Ethan had given those orders, too.

"Keep your head down and get these horses moving!" Torregrossa edged down some, but there wasn't enough room for two in that boot.

Danny snapped the reins sharply and let out a wild whoop as the heavy animals jumped against the traces and pounded forward with all the force of a juggernaut.

A gun cracked up ahead. Danny cut loose with another yell, and the team, pulling the stage, threw up their heads, running against their bits, eyes rolling. Danny held them steady in a direct line for the man in the middle. He could not have stopped them now if his life had depended on it. And maybe it did.

The kid glanced up at Ethan as the experienced gunman matched the sway of his body to the sway of the coach, shotgun in his hands, rifle within reach as the horses thundered down the road.

"Keep 'em steady! Don't let them break stride!"

No danger there, Danny thought as he strained every muscle in his shoulders, arms, and hands, to keep some control over the hard-running animals. Sweat bathed his face and threatened his grip on the lines, but he clenched his fists tighter and held on.

Up ahead a startled cry penetrated the thunderous tattoo

of the coach's wheels. The outlaws broke as a bullet whistled past Ethan's ear. From inside the coach a single six-gun answered them, and, outside, Torregrossa's shotgun kicked against his shoulder as it coughed out its deadly load in a violent spasm.

One of the men, out of the way of the hurling stagecoach, drew a steady bead on Torregrossa only to catch the full force of the gunman's load. It sent him somersaulting off the rear of his horse as the animal bolted from beneath him. Astride his horse next to the fallen man, another had been drawing a careful bead on Ethan but caught part of the same load as the buckshot scattered. A smaller man than the first, this one yelped and grabbed for his left shoulder and arm as small, red blotches blossomed the length of his sleeve. He wasn't out, not yet, but it would take him a few moments to recover himself, and Ethan used those seconds to shift the shotgun, searching for the third member of the bunch with his second barrel while the six-gun inside the coach cracked continually with an unbroken rhythm. Ethan grinned just a little, the ice of battle sliding through his veins.

The fellow inside the coach added to the confusion and kept the outlaws guessing, wondering where the next slug was going to hit, but Torregrossa didn't figure there was much chance of hitting anything without the spread of the shotgun pattern. The marksmanship of the man inside the coach didn't give Hawk any surprises as he shifted his aim with the scatter-gun, and again it roared as the coach careened past the decimated bunch.

The third outlaw, square and burly, was already behind in the dust. But, untouched by the contents of the shotgun's second blast, he now lunged his horse after the coach in earnest pursuit. He only came on for several lengths, throwing hot lead after the coach in a futile display, before abruptly drawing up his horse and turning back to join his wounded companions.

"How you doin', kid?" Ethan bellowed above the horrendous noise of the coach in full flight. He cracked open the shotgun, threw the spent shells over the side, and reloaded the weapon all in one swift motion. He hadn't even reached for the rifle and didn't intend to as he glanced over his shoulder, face set and stony, assuring himself the outlaws had not taken up the pursuit again.

Danny was too busy attempting to reassert his control over the terrified horses as he hauled himself back up on the driver's box to answer.

"Whoa, up there!" Danny yelled the command to the team in a muleskinner's voice and placed a boot on the powerful foot brake on his right. He was a skinny kid, but he knew horses, and he used the power of command to aid him. "Ease off there, boys! Pull it up!"

By degrees, Danny managed to shorten their strides, sweating at the thought of what would happen if a wheel dropped into an unexpected pothole in the old road and rolled the coach. Hands wrapped in the leather of the reins, cut and bleeding by the fierceness of his battle with the team, Danny was almost standing upright in the driver's seat. The muscles corded in his arms, shoulders, neck, and legs as he finally brought the now tired animals to a halt. He looped the reins around the brake and let them blow, casting a sidelong glance at his companion.

Ethan reached beneath the driver's seat and pulled out the canteen. "Want a drink?"

There was blood mixed with sweat on Danny's hands, but these injuries were minor. When he accepted the canteen from his partner, he could still hear the singing of the bullets as they had passed dangerously close. The guttural roar of the shotgun still boomed in his ears, and the sharp cracks of the .45s beat counterpoint to the maddened pounding of the horses' hoofs.

The kid wiped his hands on his pants and drank deeply, not even noticing the metallic staleness of the water. He'd done okay. He had guided the team even through the worst of it. He'd managed to hold them steady, but the whole time he had been tinglingly aware the sturdy luggage boot that had surrounded him would not be capable of stopping a bullet.

Still, he was a little self-conscious. Ethan hadn't raised a sweat. In fact, he did not look any different than he might if he had been out sparking in a buggy on a spring afternoon. Danny wondered if he could have remained perched up on top in clear view as calmly as Torregrossa had when the lead had gotten thick. He did not know. And, he could not decide at the moment whether it had been courage, foolhardiness, or merely the inability to be elsewhere that had kept Ethan on the driver's box, wielding his shotgun. Regardless, the kid wondered what it would take to cultivate such an exterior.

"I better walk 'em out," Danny said, handing the canteen back to Ethan. Then he picked up the reins, clucked to the sweat-frothed horses, and got them moving at a slow pace.

The coach gave a small lurch, then started rolling.

"I believe, sir," a voice called from the coach below, "that we have put them to rout, and victory is ours."

Ethan chuckled, propped the shotgun beside his knee, and reached over the side to firmly clasp the man's hand. Tension was easing off, the knot of nerves unwound in his chest, and he could draw long, even breaths again. His cool façade hid the agitation of the battle and the let-down after. Always, it was the same when it was over, and he took stock. The first critical moments when all danger was past were like a pause in time. And then it sank in. Often men were dead. This time they were at least wounded. Other men. Not himself. It was an unbidden, long look into the abyss of eternity.

Life took on new dimensions each time he faced death. Senses sharpened, nerves of steel locked down without conscious thought, but on the surface he remained cold and detached, displaying only an icy gaze and steady gun hand. When it was over, it crumbled away bit by bit, leaving him strangely satisfied, but oddly empty, the fighting blood still sizzling through his veins.

Ethan glanced over his shoulder as the stage moved smoothly along. "Can't be sure our friends won't be following."

"I think that greener of yours pretty much took the fight out of 'em for now," Danny said.

"You're probably right, but it pays a man to be cautious."

Danny flipped the reins, picking up the pace just a little when the horses' sides calmed to easier breathing. "Never saw anybody less cautious in my life." The admiration was thick and strong in his voice.

Ethan cast Danny a sideways glance, then let his gaze wander to the surrounding countryside, slipping past. "Danny, I didn't do any more than what had to be done. How much of a chance do you think we would have had back there if I hadn't had the shotgun?"

Danny shrugged. "You also had my rifle and a hand gun."

"They would have nailed us, Danny. We were sitting ducks and no more than just plain lucky that they didn't think of shooting the horses. And the only reason they didn't was because I was blasting away with the shotgun. Caught 'em flat-footed. A double-barreled shotgun is about the best equalizer I can think of. Think of your own hide first, Danny. It's the only one you've got."

"Like you looked after yours that day I almost got hung?"

"It almost got me killed," Torregrossa countered. "I'll carry the scar for my trouble, and I wasn't myself then."

Danny snorted. "You'd do it again."

He said it with such certainty and conviction that it rattled the gunman and gave him pause to think, because he had to admit to himself that the boy was right. Not too long before that he would not have done anything at all to save the boy. He would certainly never have given a moment's thought to letting a kid partner up with him. It was probably the most dangerous thing he had ever done. Especially with a cocky kid much like he had been in his own youth.

Torregrossa turned a cold-eyed stare on Danny, but the kid did not even blink. *Cocky little bastard,* Ethan thought to himself, just like the sort of son he might have produced had he ever married and settled down.

"My brains were scrambled for longer than I care to think about."

"Uhn-huh."

Ethan shifted on the seat as the horses, benefiting from their restive pace, picked it up again under Danny's guidance. He had never been a man to duck the truth. And the fact was, though he had not given serious thought to it, he would risk his neck again for the kid, a boy he would never have known if he had not taken that unexpected dive off the Mississippi paddle wheeler.

"I might do it again," Ethan admitted, "if I wasn't too far away, or already lying half dead behind some rock. But if you want to stay alive, Danny, don't count on it. Don't *ever* count on it."

Chapter Thirteen

In his room above the saloon, Torregrossa was sprawled on his back on the lumpy bed, staring up at the ceiling. The kid was down in the saloon, looking for a beer, while he was regarding the paint, peeling in chips and curls above him. The prone position was, Ethan had discovered years before, the best position for thinking, and he had a lot to think about. A part of him noted the room had long needed a fresh whitewashing, and the curtains were faded, though the room itself was surprisingly clean, and another part was focused right where it was needed. The Burr Line and its troubles. It was a puzzle. All of the pieces were there, but they just weren't fitting together as they should.

There had not been any further attempt on the stage after the encounter on the road. With first light they would be heading back to Stillwater. Ethan expected more trouble, but he wasn't sure that the source behind it was Sam Reo. In fact, the more he thought about it, the more he was positive Reo *wasn't* behind it. It made no sense, a man of his cut, taking the risks it appeared he was, to wrest from its owner something as unprofitable as now was the Burr Line. Sam Reo had been on that ridge — there was no denying it — but he had appeared to be looking for something, and Torregrossa knew for a fact he had not been among the attackers who had tried to waylay the stage.

Below, subtle changes, signaling the transition of saloon life from late afternoon to early evening, were growing louder. Glass clinked against glass and thudded softly on felt covered table tops where men were sitting down together for a game of cards. The piano player took his place at the end of the bar and started banging out tunes that rose above the swelling bedlam of the establishment. Voices continued to grow louder as night came on, and some of the cowhands managed to put away quickly more than enough drinks to add to the boisterousness. Additionally, it was Saturday night. Everything the countryside had to offer would wander through the saloon before the night was through. Ethan wasn't interested in going downstairs, but he had promised to meet Danny there after he had gone to their room, stashed their gear, and cleaned up.

It was about that time. The kid was a good fellow, but he still lacked the savvy that could keep him out of a real jam. Ethan climbed to his feet and crossed the room to the wash basin, splashing some water into it from a pitcher, using it to wash away earlier thoughts in favor of more personal ones. Rona. She was a strong woman, full of fight, but not quite certain how to take on this fight and win. He had liked her the instant they'd met. Tyler Harding was apparently her right-hand man, and another matter altogether.

Torregrossa lifted more water to his face, then straightened, grabbed the rag of a towel provided on the rack, and scrubbed it against his beard-roughened skin. He didn't believe for a minute Harding was the man he first appeared to be. Plenty of men involved with the Burr Line were dead, including Rona's brother, Hank. Harding had supposedly appointed himself Rona's protector and counsel. He had stuck with her like a burr caught in a horse's mane. So, why was he alive? For that matter, though Ethan loathed to think about it, why was Rona still alive?

He tossed the towel aside and started for the door. The attack on the coach had failed. Sam Reo was still around Stillwater, as was Tyler Harding, and, no doubt, whoever had been responsible for the attack on the coach. So was Rona. The stage, he decided, was going to make record time rolling back to Stillwater.

He felt he best get Danny out of the saloon. They would need a good night's rest, considering the trail back. Besides, the kid had a dodger out on him in another state. Hard to tell how far a thing like that might spread and how fast. A price on his head put there by his own stepfather and riding with Ethan Torregrossa — the boy didn't need much more than that. And, still, there was the matter of his own loss of sight. The loss had not slowed him down much up on top of that stagecoach, but he had had a shotgun in that scrape. He had not been pressed yet with a hand gun, at least not since Danny's near hanging, and that was all in a blurry past.

Ethan exited the room, pocketed the key, and strode down the hall, while reflecting on his own life. There had been a time, not very long ago, when he would have arrived in Stillwater with his assignment, taken in the situation at a glance, and torn into it, giving the people a first-hand lesson that there was more to fear in this world than the Sam Reos who occupied it. There were also the Ethan Torregrossas, a different breed entirely. That was his past, yet he felt distanced from it now, as if it had been another man performing those deeds, and he had been but an interested spectator. Something had changed. He wasn't certain what had triggered it, the bullet crease in his skull, his partial blindness, or perhaps Danny. Whatever it was, he bore the same name as when he had boarded the *River Hawk*, had the same reputation, and that reputation meant trouble. Only he was not the same man.

He silently trod the sparsely carpeted hall to where it opened onto a balcony overlooking the saloon below and paused, casting about for Danny. It was ironic that only a short time before he had been searching with unrelenting resolve for his own past. Trying to find out who he had been, eager to step back into his identity, only to discover that, once he had found himself, he was no longer the man he sought. Where he had expected to step back into his identity like it was a suit of well-fit, comfortable clothes, he found instead only shreds. He had changed. And, more importantly, he liked the changed Ethan Torregrossa better than he liked what he had been. He could not go back. He could only go forward to what was yet to be.

Sounds and smells drifted up to him from below as he squinted his good eye against the haze of rising smoke. Finally he spied the kid at the far end of the bar, a beer hardly touched, sitting on the polished wood before him. His rifle was cradled in his right arm, barrel pointed toward the floor.

Good instincts, Ethan decided, then hesitated a moment longer and checked to make sure his gun slid smoothly in its holster before starting down the stairs. He was a few risers down when Danny caught sight of him, grinned, and lifted his mug of beer in salute. But Ethan wasn't focused primarily on the boy. His instincts for survival were finely honed and with good reason. Because of that, half blind or not, he was aware when the batwings swung open and three men swaggered inside.

It took only an instant, but recognition dawned, and the warm, open expression Ethan had been wearing in greeting for Danny faded and hardened into deep lines and an icy stare. That black, moonlit night aboard the river boat came back in a rush. That and a hell of a lot more. He knew those three brothers, knew them well. He had been hired to clean up a town in Texas. The pay had been good, his methods not questioned. A wild bunch had been hoorawing the town, forcing the people to pay for protection by them until someone had come up with the idea of sending for Ethan Torregrossa. Where there had been five brothers then, there were now only three, any of whom would kill him in an eye blink, given the opportunity. There had been a considerable number of other cutthroats running in their pack in Texas. Ethan had lured them into town, cornered them, and demanded their surrender. They had reacted the way he had anticipated, but from his secured position it had been like shooting fish in a barrel when he returned fire. When it was over, better than half of them were dead or wounded. One of the brothers had been among the dead. Another died of his wounds a short time later. The other three had scattered and run, breaking free and clearing out of town. And now they were here.

Ethan came down the last couple of steps into the crowded saloon and, with a gunfighter's caution, remained within the clutch of people, one of many. He watched the newcomers closely to make sure the three Cade brothers were alone. Odds could change mighty quickly, and he had a score to settle that he did not intend to let slide. The peculiar chill that preceded a fight blossomed in his belly and spread throughout his body. It swept away hot anger, leaving in its place a chilled void.

He was edging his way through the crowd when he saw one of the brothers fix on Danny, who was standing in a bright pool of light cast by an oil lamp directly overhead, then jab one of his other brothers in the ribs. They exchanged a few words, and all three stared at the kid. Then they were boxing him, one leaning on the bar directly in front of him, as Danny came alert. But it would have been too late had Ethan not been approaching from the flank.

"Sure looks like a face I got on my poster," a sandy-haired, gap-toothed Cade brother announced, rummaging in his vest pocket for the paper. "What say you stand right where you are while I do me some checkin'," he drawled in what amounted to a command to Danny who had stiffened and straightened, hand tightening on the rifle in his arms.

"Hell, he ain't nothin' but a kid," a second, shorter, heavier Cade remarked from behind Danny to let their prey know there was more than one of them. "We can take him slick as hog grease."

Ethan's last steps brought him to within earshot.

"He's riding with me."

"Well, hell, mister, that don't mean there ain't a poster out on him," the sandy-haired Cade said without casting a glance in Ethan's direction. "And if there is, we aim to. . . ." He left the sentence unfinished as he half turned and his eyes came to rest on Torregrossa.

Ethan's blue-steel eyes glittered beneath black eyebrows, and he waited.

"You're dead!" the sandy-haired Cade brother said fiercely as if the conviction in his voice alone would make it true.

Ethan shrugged and smiled grimly. "You had your chance. Now it's my turn."

Other patrons of the saloon were beginning to smell trouble and edged away. A growing silence curled out from them across the room in a wave. Danny was rigid. The pungent smell of too much booze and stale smoke filled Ethan's nostrils, and he felt each lungful of stagnant air that he drew.

He was tinglingly aware that he walked very close to death in those moments. The three Cade brothers weren't particularly good, but they did outnumber him, and he was less than what he had been when they had last met. He counted it in his favor that they did not know that. He looked at Danny. The kid was ready to use that rifle.

"You got more lives than a damn' cat!" the youngest of

109

the brothers, directly behind Danny, complained to Hawk. "We checked everywheres! You have to be dead."

"Don't be an ass, little brother," the middle Cade snarled, and that was all he said. Not one for making speeches or worrying about explanations, he was going for his gun.

Ethan saw it, and his own gun was already coming up out of his holster in a movement smoothly oiled by time and practice. The only problem was — Danny was right in the middle.

No strangers to this kind of trouble, saloon patrons were scattering, none of them caring to risk collecting a bullet meant for another. Saloon girls screamed, and tables and chairs scraped against the sand-gritted wooden floor, being thrown out of the way in someone's haste to reach cover.

Ethan felt the hard coolness of the gun butt in his hand and sensed, more than saw, Danny move as time dragged into slow motion. Then, just as abruptly, time shot forward again, and Danny's rifle barrel whipped across the youngest Cade's midsection with brutal force, sending him crashing to the floor with a blood-freezing yelp of malice and pain as Danny dropped in anticipation of Torregrossa's six-gun.

Cool steel cradled in Ethan's palm spat hot lead, the slug taking the brother between himself and Danny just off center. Blood spattered the man's shirt, and he spun half around, reeling into the bar past Danny as the gun dropped from his hand to the floor with a solid thump. He followed it down without a sound.

The near collision cost Danny his balance, and he half stumbled, half fell to one knee, bringing the business end of his rifle around to center on the remaining member of the trio still on his feet — the eldest and deadliest of the surviving Cade brothers.

A bullet whipped close by Ethan's side, but its nearness

was not a distraction to the experienced, and Torregrossa shifted his aim from the first target to this one. He had to hand it to the kid — he was down, possibly wounded, Ethan couldn't tell — but he was valiantly trying to wield his rifle in the tight quarters. Ethan's six-gun moved faster. By rights, Ben, the eldest Cade, should have had him, and no one knew that better than he did. But the infuriated manhunter and outlaw was in too much of a hurry. His shots went wide, whipping past Ethan like angry hornets. Torregrossa's thoughts were of Danny, and he did not miss.

Danny checked the impulse to pull the trigger on his rifle as the last Cade fell, a curse on his lips.

An odd, squeezing sensation crawled in the pit of Ethan's stomach as he turned to give Danny the full benefit of his good eye, not certain until he focused on the boy whether he had been hit or had sought the floor out of good sense when the lead had begun flying. The apprehensive feeling vanished instantly when he saw his partner, struggling to his feet between the fallen brothers, one unmoving, one seriously wounded, and one gasping and clutching at his gut where the kid's rifle barrel had solidly caught him. Torregrossa shifted his field of sight back and forth across the remaining Cades and counted it as over. At the same moment, he realized he had changed even more than he had guessed. All his life, he had lived only for himself. It was soul shaking, but during the past seconds he had put Danny's life above his own.

Rifle swinging in his hand, barrel again pointing toward the floor, Danny crossed the few feet of blood-splattered floor as the sheriff, a tall, rangy, ramrod of a man, sporting a little snow on the roof and carrying at the ready a dependable scatter-gun, stormed in through the batwings.

"It was self-defense, Sheriff," Ethan heard someone say stridently above the low, anxious hum of conversation that

111

surged around them as the sounds of gunfire died. "That fella in the middle drew on the other 'n' first."

"Get these men to a doc." The sheriff tossed out the order. He glanced at Ethan and Danny, his brown-eyed gaze cold as winter's first breath. "You brought the stage in from Stillwater."

Torregrossa nodded. Danny frowned and tensed.

The sheriff flicked the kid a hard glance, but it was the set of the older, dark-skinned man who kept his attention. There was one dangerous man, no doubt about it.

"Don't like it, but I'll take the word of the folks here." The sheriff made it his business to keep order in his town, but he was no fool. He was not as fast as he used to be, and any man fast enough to take on the Cade brothers would be able to nail his hide to the barn door. Nonetheless, such a man was not a desirable element to have in his town.

"Stage pulls out again at dawn?" the sheriff probed.

Ethan couldn't help grinning at the lawman's obvious meaning. "We'll be driving it back to Stillwater," he assured him. Then he paused, letting that sink in. "Probably won't be back till next week's run." He enjoyed riding the town's protector a bit, and the smile he gave him was probably enough to make the man figure him for crazy.

Carson City's sheriff nodded and gave a grunt as a couple of citizens collected the youngest Cade, ushering him outside. "You're new around here, but seein' as how you're both rightly employed, I'll be expecting you to stir up less trouble on your next trip."

"Seems a fair expectation," Ethan said agreeably, and Danny just lifted a shoulder.

"We're riding for the line," Danny said. "The line has trouble, so do we. We ain't looking for it, Sheriff, but we'll do what we have to to keep our hides whole."

"Kid talks real good," the lawman acknowledged. "But that don't change what I just said."

He followed the youngest of the Cades outside, batwings flapping shut behind him.

Chapter Fourteen

Rona looked back over her shoulder at the load the heavy freight wagon carried, assuring herself it was riding smoothly, then smiled once more at Jake's expertise at packing the supply of heavy timbers, food staples, spools of fuse, boxes of dynamite, and heavy wire. Nothing moved or jostled in counterpoint with the lumbering gait of the wagon. She was convinced she could transport nitroglycerin up that mountain with no danger to herself if it were Jake who had packed it.

Her gloved hands holding the reins with experienced deftness, Rona now glanced up at the sky, her wrists propped on her knees. She'd make it to Karl Schmidt's mine well before dark, and that was the way she preferred it, considering the narrowness of the old mine road and the steepness of the dropoffs it crawled along. The wagon rumbled with muted thunder, the harnesses jingling, and the sturdy draft horses clomped in contented rhythm.

It wasn't unusual for Karl to send a message down the mountain, asking the freight line to bring up a shipment of needed supplies. And Karl's mine was showing steady color. He paid upon delivery without complaint, gave her food and lodging for the night, and then she headed downhill with the coming of the next day's sun. Rona was grateful Karl harrumphed away the troubles the Burr Line had endured and continued to give his business to her.

He was one of the few who still did. Money was getting

tight, and she was becoming worried. She was working her way through the small nest egg her father had left upon his death, and, when it was gone, that would be the end. She had considered giving up, holding on to what was left, liquidating the line's assets, and moving on. But what would she find for herself beyond the Burr Line? Rona did not consider herself the marrying and settling-down type. She couldn't cook more than subsistence meals and didn't think of herself as a mother. She loved what she was doing. It was possible she could get a new start somewhere else. With the right hired hands she could make a go of it. She balked at the idea of leaving Stillwater, having spent her entire life in its environs, but there was part of her that was realistic enough to accept change. The other part, however, railed at the injustice and demanded restitution for all she had suffered. That same aspect of her personality shuddered and refused to accept the victory of the forces taking the Burr Line apart, at the destruction of her dream of extending it. It meant, in her eyes, the triumph of Sam Reo.

The mere thought of losing this fight made her snap the lines, sending the team along at a brisker pace. She regretted the action immediately, though, and drew them back. This was no road to travel in a hurry. Once the horses were quieted and again settled into their even, ground-eating pace, Rona leaned back on the seat and determinedly focused her thoughts in another direction, and that was toward her new shotgun rider and stage driver.

They were making excellent time back to Stillwater, the heavy stage rocking on its springs as it came around a particularly blind curve. Torregrossa was rocking in rhythm with his shotgun propped on his thigh, muzzle pointed skyward. Once they were uneventfully past that curve, Ethan scanned the horizon in all directions, saw nothing, and relaxed just a little.

Danny clucked to the team, picking up the pace a bit, and looked over at Ethan.

"Eager to get back, ain't you?"

"Pieces just don't fit. I need to spend some time in that town."

"Sure you ain't thinkin' about our freight?"

Ethan grinned, remembering how he had fast-talked the owner of the saloon, who had several bottles of aged good whiskey to be sent to a saloon in Stillwater, into sending the precious shipment with them. He had pledged the Burr Line would stand good for any loss, which meant, as far as he was concerned, that *he* would stand good for it, since he had made the promise without the clearance of the Burr Line's owner. "That, too."

The stage rumbled along, Danny and Ethan riding now in companionable silence, each with his own thoughts. The road lay clear ahead, and, if there were no trouble, they would arrive back in Stillwater early.

"You wonder why this Reo fella wants to tear down the Burr Line like he's been doin'?" Danny raised the question as the team leaned into the pull for the next hill.

"Doesn't make much sense to me," Torregrossa admitted. "Rona seems to think he wants to take it over."

"Not much left to take over the way it's been chewed up."

"That's my feeling. Did you see the way Ty Harding and Sam Reo looked at each other when we were leaving Stillwater?"

"Didn't take any notice."

"Looked like they wanted to tear each other's hearts out."

"Seems reasonable, from what Rona says."

"It was more personal than that. It was between *them*."

Danny looked at Ethan. "What're you sayin'?"

"There's something going on there. I think the two of them brought it with 'em, and now Rona's caught in the middle. When Harding looked at Reo, he didn't just want him stopped, he wanted to see the man's blood coloring the streets. Reo didn't look at Harding much differently."

With a low whistle, Danny shook his head, urged the team on with a light slap of the reins, and guided them into the last leg of the trip into Stillwater. When they rolled in, great clouds of dust rolling up behind the wheels, Danny slowed the horses abruptly, nearly standing on the brake to bring the stage to a halt in front of the stage office.

Rona was nowhere in sight. That wasn't right, and Torregrossa didn't have to know her long to know that for truth. The sound of the stagecoach's approach would have brought her out into the street to see that all was well. There had been too much bad news for her to ignore the coach's arrival.

Ethan jumped lightly over the side as the conveyance swayed to a stop, heading for the door before Danny could even tie off the reins. At his approach the heavy wooden door swung wide, and Ty Harding stood framed in the opening, face etched in lines of worry, his left arm cradled in a sling. One booted foot on the boardwalk, the other still in the dusty street, Torregrossa took it all in, and it didn't set right.

"Where's Rona?"

Somewhere along the road back from Carson City Ethan had accepted the reality that the stage wasn't going to draw the trouble in returning that it had had on the trip out. That had meant only one thing to him. Something else had to be the target, *someone* else, and to his way of thinking that could only be Rona.

"She took the freight wagon out," Ty said. "I tried to stop

her, but we got a special order to haul up to the Schmidt mine. He's a good customer, and she's done it before. I'd've gone with her, but I tore up my shoulder, helping with the loading."

"You let that little lady go out alone?" Danny accused as he drew up alongside Torregrossa, shoving his hat back on his head, and swinging that rifle of his like it was little more than a hand gun.

"Kid," Harding said derisively, "you don't stop Rona once she's got her mind set."

"How long ago did she leave?" Ethan asked the question.

"Couple of hours. I'd have gone along, even like this, but she wasn't having any of it."

"Saddle our horses," Ethan shot the command at Danny, eyes still fastened on Ty's face as the kid turned and ran, without comment, to ready the mounts. "What road did she and that wagon take?"

"Old mining road starts a couple of miles east of town. Swings due north, then cuts up into the hills. It's a good day's drive up there in that freight wagon. The old codger she's hauling for was a friend of her father's. Claims to have hit a new vein and needs them new timbers in a hurry."

Tyler Harding had been watching the gunman and his young companion, appraising them. He turned his latest plan over in his mind and decided it still wasn't lacking. That lone drive Rona was on would settle things permanently between himself and Sam Reo. He had a welcoming rock slide all set for Rona. When hell broke loose, the woman would be killed, and Sam Reo would end up dangling from the end of a rope for her murder. The evidence would be irrefutable.

He had not planned on Hawk and the kid getting back so soon, but maybe it was a helpful turn of events. They were hot to go after her, but she had enough of a lead that they

118

would not be able to get to her before she reached the rigged rock slide. Maybe they would be the ones to find her body and the evidence incriminating Sam Reo. That would fit in very nicely.

Ethan watched Harding's face closely while Danny hustled the horses. There was a lot going on behind those piercingly black eyes and that deceivingly round, open face.

"Maybe you couldn't have stopped her, but you could have followed."

Harding's face froze into set lines, eyes glittering, and he did not choose to respond before Danny, astride his horse, rounded the corner, Torregrossa's mount on lead. Danny dropped the reins into his partner's hands, then sat back in the saddle, eyes fixed on Rona's hired hand.

"We better get a move on, Ethan. She's putting distance between us."

Harding flinched at the kid's utterance of Torregrossa's name. He had had his suspicions since that gun play a few days back. It had been too slick, too good. Too much like what Hank Burr had described to him as the talent of the gunman he had hired, Ethan Torregrossa. Hank had played right into his hands, telling him that. Torregrossa's reputation, from what Harding had heard, cut a mighty wide swath.

The pair of horses were eager for the trail, stamping their impatience. Ethan swung into the saddle, leather creaking sharply as it took his weight. His rifle was jammed into the boot alongside his knee, and he allowed the palm of his hand to linger on the stock, pinning Harding with a penetrating gaze. He knew the instant that Danny had let the name *Ethan* slip Harding had made the connection between the name and the gunman Hank had hired.

"You be here when we get back," Ethan warned Harding. "I wouldn't like being forced to look for you."

Torregrossa and Danny turned their horses as one, putting them to the road out of town at a gallop. Neither looked back.

Tyler Harding was doing enough staring for all of them. Tiny beads of perspiration broke out across his forehead and above his lip as the rapid tattoo of hoofbeats echoed off into the distance. The kid had thrown him off for a moment — Ethan Torregrossa's reputation for solitary work was at odds with his having a young partner — but Harding had no doubts now. Turning, he ducked back inside the stage office when Jake came running from the hotel restaurant to tend to the dragging and lathered horses. He ducked out of the unneeded sling, stretched his arm expansively a couple of times, wincing against the sting of healing buckshot wounds, then headed out the back door.

The kid and Torregrossa had caught him flat-footed when he and his boys had tried to take the stage on the trail, but it would not happen again. Now that he knew what he was up against, Harding figured a slight change in plans would make his life that much simpler. With the plan already in motion, all he had to do was be in the right place at the right time.

Harding saddled his horse in record time, smiling wickedly to himself. He knew Reo wasn't yet aware that it had been Ty's gun that had crippled the young banker, Clay Reo, during the course of a robbery. But it was just a matter of time, and Reo's presence made him uncomfortable, to say the least. His plan would get rid of Reo, and unfortunately Rona had a definite rôle in the drama. Her blatant distrust of Reo had played right into Harding's hand. All he had had to do over the last several months was to arrange more accidents. Rona had a one-track mind. And it would be thanks to Rona that Harding would soon be free of Reo.

He vaulted into the saddle, catching a handful of mane and reins, and galloped out of Stillwater. He knew where his men were waiting, and he knew every shortcut in the country thanks to Rona's father who had traced the various trails for Harding over the brief period he had worked for Joseph Burr. He rode like there was a demon astride his shoulder, and there were many in his past who would testify that image was not far from the truth.

Sam Reo picked his way through the back country with anticipation. Finally, vengeance was in his grasp. Tyler Harding. He now knew that Harding had been one of the robbers of his brother's bank as had been indicated in the letter he had found waiting for him upon his return to Stillwater. Over the last two years Reo had sifted through many aliases in his pursuit of the man who had shot his brother in the back. Yet, until now, Harding appeared to be a man without a past.

The bastard who had shot his brother had not left behind so much as a line drawing to go along with the posters that offered rewards. Sam Reo had been determined from the beginning that there must be no mistake when he took down the man responsible for making his brother an invalid. And he had no intention of involving the authorities. To hell with the law's need for evidence. He could not leave this to the coolness of the law's regard. Revenge was his to levy, and he wanted the misbegotten son-of-a-bitch to know exactly why he was dying and who was doing the killing.

Reo remembered the helpless state in which he had left his brother, and he remembered, clearly, his own history. It wasn't pretty, and it wasn't much to be proud of, but it sure as hell qualified him to seek revenge. For months — almost a year and a half — he had pursued the nameless, faceless outlaw, guided by hints and rumors, with the help of the outlaw's enemies, and sometimes with the aid of miraculous good luck. When he had encountered Harding in Stillwater, for an instant he had thought he had found his man. But nothing was known about him, and Harding had insinuated himself into the good graces of the Burr family. Reo was left again with uncertainty. He had requested information on Harding, but until now there had been nothing to go on. The passage of time had nearly driven him beyond his capacity for patience.

Now he could taste it — revenge. In town, he had learned that the freight wagon had gone out on a run with Rona driving. Since both her newest hands were on the Carson City run with the stage — something he had verified by making sure with his own eyes — he had naturally assumed that Tyler Harding would be riding shotgun with Rona.

Harding slowed his mount, took a couple of hillocks at an easy gallop, crossed one of the numerous streams that ran down off the mountains, then slowed his horse even more as he entered a stretch of land littered with large rocks and deep potholes. Old man Burr had taken him this way more than once before he had fallen ill. Harding drew his horse up to a slow walk, and the animal picked his way through the débris. The slow pace got under the rider's skin, but he knew he would be able to make it up on the other side where the land rolled into a basin before stepping up into the higher mountains. His three men would be waiting in a mote of trees on the far side of the basin.

He imagined Torregrossa finding what was left of Rona and the freight wagon and recalled the bald-faced demand the man had made that he be at the Burr office when he returned. If his reputation was anything to go by, Ethan Torregrossa would be as dangerous as a teased snake, but he wouldn't be expecting to see Tyler Harding in these hills, and that was what would give Harding the advantage. That was the edge that would leave him the only one standing when this day drew to a close.

Rona Burr would be dead, a regrettable waste that couldn't be helped. Torregrossa and that kid would be dead as well, having been killed by Sam Reo, whom Ty himself would be forced to kill after stumbling on the scene when it was too late. He would have to forfeit the pleasure of seeing the single-minded, half-crazed Reo swing, but Harding was a practical man. The current plan would have to do, and it would leave no reason for that gutless sheriff in Stillwater to doubt his word.

He kicked his horse into a run as they cleared the rocky, pitted patch of earth and nosed him a little more to the northeast, across the green and rolling valley that skirted the edge of the badlands on one side and the higher mountains on the other. He would warn his men about the unbending, merciless presence of Ethan Torregrossa. Forewarned, they would take him down.

Chapter Fifteen

Both Ethan and Danny were pushing their horses hard. The animals were of a pair — two tough and stringy range ponies used to hard work and rough country. Ethan had sympathy for the laboring beasts, but even stronger was the urge to press on, to catch up with Rona atop the freight wagon, lumbering up the old mining road. There was an unsettled, uncomfortable feeling in the pit of his belly, an old companion he recognized silently to himself — fear. Few would have credited Torregrossa with an anxious moment in his life. But he felt trepidation now, and had known it as a companion since his childhood.

What was going on with the Burr Line was all wrong, and worse, he was making mistakes. He had known it the moment he and Danny had ridden away from Tyler Harding. It had been a mistake to leave the man alone, and standing.

When he had been a youngster on the plantation, the butt of constant teasing and abuse from the other children, Ethan had been aware of his parentage. His mother had been a quadroon, his father the owner of the vast plantation. Ethan, by dint of early and brutal experience, had known how to take his enemies down and keep them there. He didn't understand, now, what had stayed his hand with Harding — and whatever it had been, he wished it had been otherwise.

"Got something on your mind?" Danny asked when they slowed their horses' pace to allow them to blow.

"Might've made a mistake, leaving Harding behind."

"Thought the same, but I don't see what you could have done short of shooting him in cold blood."

"There are ways to prod a man, Danny." The heaviness of Ethan's Southern drawl colored his words. "It didn't have to be cold blood."

Ethan gave Danny a long, cool look that said it all.

The kid shook his head. "We would have lost time."

"I know," Torregrossa agreed. "But that wasn't the reason why I held back."

"Then what was it?"

"Don't know, kid," the gunman answered out loud, and then, silently to himself, added: *and that's what makes it feel like someone stuck cold steel in my chest.*

The climb was steep, the drop-off alongside the mining road something Rona avoided looking into as she continued the ascent. This was the roughest part of the drive up the old road, and the team was working hard.

"Steady on, boys," she called softly to the horses, leaning into the traces. "Gee up, Dusty! Pull a leg, Big Dan, we're almost there."

The wagon lumbered on, the eight horses pulling with all their strength as they approached the curve. They were making good time, the stout draft horses sweating, but not overly lathered. Karl would be surprised to see them arrive so early in the day. She held the reins firmly, calling out encouragement and advice to the straining horses, blotting the sweat from her forehead with the back of one gloved hand.

She didn't know why, but, as the wagon rumbled up the road, Rona felt more and more uneasy. And that nervousness telegraphed itself to the horses through the lines. They snorted, tossing their heads, hoofs digging into the hardpan of the road's surface. She held the pace steady, eyes flicking first one way, then the other, checking the surrounding countryside for anything that might signal danger. She was looking for a figure in the brush or a highwayman in the road, not what was actually waiting for her.

In fact, she never saw it at all. She felt it. A sinking, drifting, sliding sensation, and when she did see, it was already too late. Undermined, the narrow road gave way as the weight of the fully loaded freight wagon rolled onto the softened section. The rear, off-side wheel sagged first, but that was just the beginning. In a movement that mimicked floundering in soft, sucking mud, the freight wagon listed to the right and started sliding backward.

The sudden terror that surged through Rona sent trembles through her arms. She fought for control, breath cramped in the back of her dry throat, and urged the horses to pull. Seconds stretched into time that was incomprehensible. She leaped to her feet, braced against the lurch of the wagon and the pull of the frightened horses against the reins.

"Gee up thar!" Rona bellowed against the rising volume of the coming disaster.

Soil and rock were sliding, wood groaning against the strain, and horses huffing and whinnying in protest at the sudden backward drag. *Dear God, they were going over the edge!*

"Pull, Dusty!" she yelled at the lead. "Lean into it! Pull!" She sucked deeply for breath when she thought to breathe, then bellowed again. "Pull!"

Her voice was becoming more strident as somewhere deep inside her the realization of what was about to happen burst into her consciousness. Still, she fought the slide, rejecting it. Heads thrust out before them, the horses' legs strained to move forward until Rona could see their trembling against the terrible weight of the wagon.

She didn't dare look down to her right as the wagon hung,

suspended between ascent and descent.

"Haw, Big Dan, pull! Get up thar, boys!" she shouted to the animals.

Mahogany-colored hair pulled free from its bindings to blow over her shoulders. Her normally round, smooth face was deeply lined in concentration and colored by the panic that threatened to take hold.

"Forward! Haw! Get it up! Pull!"

Her sharp words cracked like a whip. The rush of sand and gravel pattered in muted counterpoint down the impossible incline as the horses snorted, slid, and whinnied. The team, hoofs unable to find solid purchase with the weight dragging them back, somehow dug in and inched the wagon ahead as the soil continued to drop from beneath the wheels. With noble effort the eight horses strained against the traces, and Rona felt the small lurch forward.

"That's it! Pull!"

Again, there was an almost imperceptible movement upward. Rona risked a faint smile through the grime and sweat accumulating on her face. She snapped the reins for encouragement and leaned forward, instinctively trying to help. She was both afraid to move and afraid not to.

"Pull!" Her voice, raw and grating, sawed through the nerve-shattering sounds of a ground-eating landslide that was gaining momentum.

Once more forward, and then, abruptly, the whole side of the road gave way, slithering from beneath the wheels of the wagon. Rona's heart dropped to her stomach. The heavy freighter hung in space, horses still straining forward, unaware of the sudden change as stone and earth rushed and rattled down the slope. Then the wagon started to slide, and this time there was no stopping it.

The horses screamed, as only animals in pain can, as they

were suddenly wrenched backward in a tangle of legs, massive bodies, and leather harnesses. Rona shouted out her fear and disbelief as a grinding, splintering crash ripped through the mountain's stillness, sending birds rising out of the treetops in a cloud.

She tried to jump clear, but it was far too late for that. The shrieks of the falling, terrified horses pierced the air already filled with the punishing roar of the wagon's descent. The freighter started to roll, and Rona was flipped from the seat to the boot beneath it as the lines danced like trained snakes, wrapping her in a strangling web, trapping her.

Ethan pulled his horse up at the awesome roar reverberating across the face of the mountain. A chill of dread swept through him, penetrating to the bone. He looked at Danny who, despite his usually cocky manner, was washed a pasty white. The crashing, splintering blast accompanying the violent separation of wood and metal was enough to cause Ethan to feel like his guts were being twisted up within him, but there were the other sounds as well. He knew too well the pitiful screams of horses in agony. They were too late. Only a freight wagon with the bulk like the one Rona had been driving could evoke a crash like that. Only something of large proportions, tumbling down a dry gulch, could raise the dusty haze that was drifting lazily up the mountainside.

"She might've jumped clear," Danny muttered in an awed whisper as the sound of the thunderous concussion began to fade out along the face of the mountain, and the dust thinned on the breeze.

Ethan let out a string of cuss words that would have sizzled bacon, slapped his heels to his mount, and sent him lunging up the narrow, twisting freight road without heed as to what could be awaiting him around the next bend. Danny was right behind as they urged their already nearly spent mounts ahead at a faster pace.

For the first time in his life of confronting just such situations, Torregrossa was chillingly aware of his own feelings. The old Torregrossa would have first frozen at the initial sounds of the crash, evaluating what he heard, then circled far around the immediate area. He would have come up on an off side to give the matter his full consideration before coming out into the open — if he came out at all. The man he had become thought only of Rona, and the fact that, if she had survived the crash of the freight wagon at all, she'd be needing help in a hurry. That fact kept his heated blood pounding through his veins and his heart thumping against his ribs.

By the time he and Danny reached the place in the road where the wagon's plunge over the side had gouged out the earth, the dust was already sifting steadily downward, veiling the needles of the pines and the leaves of the trees. It wafted into their faces, forcing tears to their eyes and touching off fits of coughing. Ethan jerked his neckerchief up over his mouth and nose. The only audible sound came from the pitiful, high-pitched wheezing of a single, surviving horse. On the back of his mount, Torregrossa couldn't see much from the road through the cloud of dust, except broken saplings and brush torn out in a raw slash that extended down the steep slope out of sight. The wagon, horses, and driver were nowhere in view.

"Rona!" Ethan called loudly, his voice echoing off across the slide site.

Danny glanced nervously around at the mountain that rose sharply on their left and plunged nearly straight down on the right. It was his turn to watch his partner's back.

There was no answer to Ethan's call save the continued

whistling whinny of an injured animal and the trickle of dirt and rock, as the earth continued to shift and settle out after the slide. It had not been one caused by natural forces such as erosion. Ethan judged a good piece of the road had been blasted out, then back-filled with rock and loose sand. When the heavily loaded conveyance had rolled onto it, it hadn't stood a chance.

Torregrossa jumped from his horse and scrambled down the scarred slope. "Find yourself some cover," he called to Danny over his shoulder. "Whoever planned this won't be too far away."

Danny nodded and was swinging a leg over his saddle when gunshots erupted from almost directly above them. They cracked loudly in the kid's ears, but hit nowhere near him as he spilled off his mount and crowded the horses tightly against the upslope of the freight road where the mountain towered above them. It took him an instant to realize the lead was not flying in his direction, but was, instead, aimed at Ethan who was clawing and belly-crawling his way through the loose dirt and rocks, searching for some sign of the Burr Line's mistress.

On the exposed upper lip of the slope, Ethan flinched as a bullet whanged off a rock, singing into the loosened earth between his fingers. As he jerked his hand back, reflex broke his precarious hold, and he slid on his belly down the slope over unstable soil and small rocks in the path of the wagon. Almost the instant he let go, the gunshots stopped, then started again as his bruising dive ground to a halt only a few yards away from the wagon. He scrambled and rolled sideways behind the shelter of a splintered tree trunk, then paused to catch his breath and glance around, searching the choppy terrain for Rona.

First, he saw only the wagon, wheels awkwardly on top, still turning, and the horses. Seven of the team of eight were dead, and the survivor's cries of pain, as it gamely struggled against the restricting harness and pressing teammates with two broken legs, made Torregrossa sick to his stomach. He drew his six-gun and quickly put an end to the animal's suffering.

With the earlier gunshots having been silenced when he had gone to ground, the single report of Ethan's weapon cracked sharply on the still air, dying away in distant echoes. It was then he heard the soft moan nearby.

"Rona!" Torregrossa bellowed into the silence, then scrambled toward the overturned wagon.

Chapter Sixteen

Ty Harding peered over the rock ledge toward the old mining road below. The sheer face of the cliff made it impossible to see much now that Torregrossa had taken cover and the kid had flattened himself against the rock face beneath the ledge. He held a rifle at the ready, and waited. Sooner or later they'd have to show themselves. When they did, he and his men would be ready.

"Keep a sharp eye," Ty said quietly to the others, positioned behind him and along the ledge.

Now that he knew he was dealing with a man of Torregrossa's reputation, he was determined neither Torregrossa nor that kid partner of his were going back to Stillwater alive. It was too dangerous to allow, and he had what he needed already. If he didn't manage to pick Sam Reo off on the face of this mountain today, the man would swing for the rigged accident. Ty would see to it. He'd been working for the Burr Line long enough now that he had a certain reputation among the folks of Stillwater. He was respectable. All he had to do was wait.

The thunderous roar of the ground-shaking crash caused Sam Reo to pull his horse up short in the midst of a steep climb, unmindful of where they were. The animal snorted, shifted and firmly planted its hoofs on the rocky soil of the hillside, and tossed its head, impatient to move on. Reo turned in the direction of the sound, listening, seeking, and finding it. His usually flat, slate-gray eyes livened, and he swung his mount off in the direction of the still grumbling mountainside.

He guided his horse up the steep slope at an angle, shifting his solidly built frame to the animal's advantage as pebbles dislodged and scattered down the grade behind them in a clattering rain. His horse dug in and lunged the last few yards, and they finally topped out above the mine road where the sound had originated.

Reo hesitated, allowing his horse to blow while he twisted in the saddle, staring down the road, then up, finally directing his gaze across rough country that appeared to go either straight up or straight down. Dust drifted in great clouds upon the wind. Sam had heard that kind of clattering roar before, and he knew it was nothing but bad news. Tyler Harding was around somewhere, and Harding was who he was after. He had to move, and it had to be fast, but he intended to come out ahead of the cold-blooded highwayman. He'd chase that bastard to hell if he had to, but it would be much better if he could end it here, on this mountain, before the sun set. He had searched and waited long enough. He would take Ty Harding down and woe be to anyone who tried to stop him.

His bay gelding was breathing easier. Sam gauged the acclivity that cut upward from the slash of a road. It was all rock, loose soil, and trees. It would be hard on the horse, but they could make it. He wheeled the pony, trotted down the road, then turned again. Kicking hard with his heels, he put the horse onto the slope at break-neck speed. Head held high, eyes wild, Reo's mount took the grade head on, half pivoting at his rider's command to choose the easier course. Momentum kept him leaping upward for several strides, and then the mountain took its toll. Reo was practically sitting on the animal's withers, but they were bogging down. The horse's lunges slowed, hoofs slipped and slid on the precipitous incline as the animal leaned forward with every ounce of its strength, legs and haunches trembling, and white froth blooming around the metal of the bit between his teeth.

Sam hated being cruel to an animal, but there was nowhere he could step down now, and the horse was teetering on the brink of falling. He slapped the reins hard across the pony's knotted haunches, dug his heels in, and the beast gave a jump that sent them up over the top. Within several more strides they found level ground.

Sam Reo stepped down from his terrified mount, pulled the rifle from its scabbard on the saddle, and started to jog along the edge, reins clasped in one hand. The horse, worn with white streaks of sweat crossing his haunches, whickered once in protest, then trotted along behind, flesh still rippling with tension beneath the surface of his blood-bay hide.

Ethan peered anxiously about, trying to see beneath the scattered timbers the wagon had been hauling and the broken brush on either side of its path of descent. Rona had not answered his call, but that did not mean she was dead. It was a litany he kept repeating to himself. *Not dead, not dead, please, not dead.* Finally he spotted her. The wagon was overturned, but one edge was lifted slightly, braced up against a large rock. She had been hidden from view by the wagon's side. Her hair, flame red where the sun flashed through it, was first to catch his attention. Even the drifting dust could not dull it enough to blend it into the dun-colored hillside. Then he spotted the pale, white arm, stripped of its sleeve, laying outstretched from beneath the sheltering wagon. Torregrossa was close enough to see the fingers curl, moving slightly.

Torregrossa had had his mettle tested time and again since childhood, and many times he had proven that there was little that could frighten him. But he had not been tested in this manner, and what was waiting for him under that wagon was something with the potential to bring him to his knees. "What've you gotten yourself into, Rona?" he muttered, holstering his gun.

Ethan stood up behind the trunk of the tree, soil loose beneath his feet, sifting down slope with a soft, sighing, hissing sound. Then, bracing one foot to control his slide, he shuffled and sidled down the steep grade toward where Rona lay.

The instant he was clear of the pine's shattered trunk the gunshots began again, but they weren't coming as fast as when he had been up near the road. And this time the volley was being answered by the sharp report of Danny's rifle. Ethan picked his way toward the wagon, rocks rolling from beneath his booted feet, earth sliding like the whole mountainside expected to cut loose again. A shot snapped past him, thudding into the upturned wooden bed of the wagon. Ethan dropped behind one of the timbers that had been scattered across the mountainside during the wagon's descent and draped himself across the part of Rona that was vulnerable to gunfire. When he turned his head and looked up the scarred slope, he spotted a man perched on the rocky ledge above the old freight road. They both froze long enough to stare across the distance into each others' eyes.

Ethan Torregrossa and Sam Reo.

If he had had Danny's rifle, he could have picked Reo right off that damned ledge. But he did not have a rifle, and the gunshots ended abruptly, echoes traveling on the stillness of the brittle air. After another moment, Reo, phantom-like, disappeared from the outcropping. Torregrossa did not see him fire again after their eyes met, and that puzzled Ethan. Almost everything about this mess confused him, and answers, what few there were, only led to more questions.

The only thing he was becoming more and more sure about was the fact that Rona might not be the real target in all this. She might be caught in some sort of crossfire. If it was otherwise, then nothing made sense at all. Reo couldn't have had a better position to lay in wait for them had he searched for an eternity, and yet he had abandoned it the instant Torregrossa had recognized him. Or, had it been the other way around? Had it been Sam Reo who had seen something he hadn't cared for? Something that hadn't set right?

Ethan saw Danny plastered up against the cut of the mining road, rifle in hand, ready to make his mark. His attention was drawn not to where Reo had been perched higher up and to the north, but rather to the south on the lower edge of the rock outcropping, towering above the mining road. Torregrossa redirected his attention, following what would be Danny's line of fire, and he spotted them. There were several men scattered along the lip, overlooking Danny's position and his own. Men Reo had brought along, perhaps. Or was it someone else?

There wasn't time for Ethan to find an answer. Rona stirred beneath him, twisting, and feebly trying to drag her arm from beneath him as if he, too, were one of the heavy timbers the wagon had been hauling when the slide took it down.

"Easy does it," Ethan whispered to her. "We're not out of the woods yet."

Danny took a chance and, holding the rifle clear of dust and rock, made his way down the scarred slide area in Ethan's footsteps, skittering, slipping, and sliding all the way.

Torregrossa levered himself up off Rona, rolled to one side, and glanced down at her face. She was fully conscious now, but, nonetheless, a distant, glazed look was in her usually bright, amber eyes. He discerned a large purpling lump on her blood-smeared forehead. Other than the lump, he spotted only a few scratches. He couldn't see any part of her body that lay beneath the heavy freighter, and he tried not to think about how she might be pinned down by the wagon.

When her eyes first focused on Ethan, Rona recognized him, but she could not fathom the fact that he had gotten the stage through to Carson City, returned, and was now hovering over her. She was confused and had to be seeing things. She told herself that confusion was normal in circumstances such as these and put all her efforts into figuring out how to extricate herself from the situation. There was one thing of which she was certain — she had heard the sounds of gunshots. Of the man hovering above her, she was not so sure.

"Just who are you anyway?" she asked Ethan. "And don't tell me you're a stage driver or shotgun rider."

There was no point in perpetuating his identity of Hawk any longer.

"Ethan Torregrossa," he told her truthfully. "Your brother sent for me."

Rona's eyes widened a bit at the revelation, but damned if she didn't nod just as if she had been expecting it.

"Anything hurt? Legs, chest?" he asked, fearing the worst.

"I feel like I've been rolled off the mountain in a barrel," she answered him, "but there's no specific pain. My legs are numb. They're stuck under the driver's seat."

Ethan's experience didn't give him much to draw on in this instance. He didn't know if her answer was good or bad.

"What about the horses?" Rona asked as she tried to pull herself up, only to discover she was immobilized by the weight of the wagon. Instead, she craned her neck to see past Ethan's shoulder.

"They're gone," Ethan told her quietly, as he searched the area for something he could use to lever the empty wagon.

"All of them?" Rona's body relaxed against the earth. There was a sizable knot in her belly, and she made no more effort to see past Torregrossa to where the valiant animals had fallen. "He's finally won then. The Burr Freight and Stage Line is finished."

Ethan studied her face for several moments. This was not a good time, but there never was. Truth was frequently a bitter pill to swallow. "The line hasn't stood a chance for some time now," he said quietly. "You've known that. You still have a coach and a good team back in Stillwater. They'll give you a stake to start over somewhere else What we have to do now is get you out of here."

To Ethan's way of thinking, the Burr Freight and Stage Line hadn't been worth too much since her brother had been killed. Maybe since before that. It had nothing to do with Rona's ability to run the business, but rather the bloody battle into which she had been sucked. As he saw it, there was no real vendetta against the business, nor had there been one against Hank, her brother, or herself. As gunshots erupted on the tableland high above the old mine road, a glimmer of understanding was beginning to dawn in Torregrossa. Shots cracked and echoed on the clear mountain air. They were loud and close, but the lead was not flying in their direction. Torregrossa glanced up as Danny slid on the seat of his pants down the last few feet of the scarred earth to the wagon. A shower of small pebbles and dirt preceded him.

There was more than one gun spitting lead along the upper slopes. Something was happening up there, and, for now at least, he, Danny, and Rona were not the center of the action. Reo was up there, but so was someone else, several persons, in fact. Guns roared and bullets ricocheted with that high-pitched whine peculiar to lead bouncing off rock.

"You OK?" Danny asked as he broke his slide by careening into one of the heavy timbers. His teeth gritted as the mammoth piece of wood shifted beneath the impact of his slight weight, so precipitous was the angle of the hillside.

Torregrossa nodded, then turned his attention once again to the wagon that pinned Rona. "Cut the harnesses loose from the horses. We're gonna have to lift the wagon and hope it'll roll," he said to Danny.

The kid braced the butt of his rifle against the wagon to keep himself from slipping even farther and glanced apprehensively over his shoulder toward the mine road.

"Sure thing."

He pulled a knife from his belt and hastened to follow Ethan's command. He slung his rifle over his shoulder by the broad strap and clambered up on top of the wagon, trying to keep doubled over, making himself as small a target as possible, then dropping over the side of the rough wooden bed to reach the fallen team. The sight of those poor, loyal beasts, broken, bloodied, and dead, tore at Danny's insides, and it wasn't easy, clinging to the steep incline, hacking away at the thick leather of the harnesses one at a time. Yet, the sturdy width of each bit of harness fell away, piece by piece, beneath the sharp sweep of his blade. What puzzled him was what had kept the wagon, horses, and Rona from crashing the rest of the way down the mountain. Only the sideways slew of the wagon's descent could explain it. A forward plunge would have taken them all down. Even now, not much held it all together. The wagon shuddered occasionally, and it occurred to Danny it might well let loose when the dead weight of the team was detached. He sure hoped Ethan knew what the hell he was doing. One wrong move and they were going to ride that wagon into hell.

Sheathing his knife, Danny crawled back over the huge, bracing timbers the crash had scattered across the face of the mountain and rejoined Torregrossa.

"What now?" he asked, breathless from his labors.

"We get this wagon rolling."

"Huh?"

Loose dirt flew in chunks and clouds as Ethan dug feverishly in a soft spot right beside Rona.

"I'm gonna get under there with her," he told Danny. "Since you cut the team free, I should be able to get enough leverage with my legs to start it moving. Once that happens, the mountain will do the rest."

He worked quickly, occasionally glancing up the hillside that rose above the freight road where the sounds of gunfire had not stilled. The frequency of the shots was dying, but some sort of exchange was still going on.

"I'll give you a hand," the kid offered, also aware of the occasional crack of gunshots.

"No," Torregrossa returned. "Keep an eye out. Sooner or later they're gonna think about us. We've got to get out of here."

Danny unslung his rifle and hunkered down, giving the slope above them a good going over, searching for any sign of movement, a sign of anything.

"Nothing that I can see," Danny said quietly, as his friend continued to work beneath the wagon.

"Good," came the grunted reply. "I'm almost ready."

"What the hell you think is goin' on up there?"

"Runnin' gunfight I'd guess. Shots are sounding more distant, not ringing so clear. But it won't be long before somebody doubles back toward us down here. Did you see anything before you came down?"

Danny shifted uncomfortably, eyes scanning the ground above them time and again. He lowered his voice. "I think I caught a glimpse of Ty Harding, but he sure wasn't alone."

"Son-of-a- . . . ," Ethan began.

"Oh, no," Rona moaned. "He's going to get himself killed out here!"

"Maybe," Torregrossa agreed, "if we're real lucky."

"How can you say that?" she asked in a puzzled tone.

"I'll explain how, if we manage to get out of here with our skins whole."

"I think you better explain now," Rona insisted.

Ethan kept on digging, widening the hollow to accommodate his shoulders. "You don't have the right of this thing, Rona," he said, as he pulled more dirt from beneath the overturned wagon. "I don't have the whole of it yet myself, but I can tell you now, you can't trust Ty Harding any further than a rabid skunk."

"But he's stuck with me through so much. . . ."

"He's probably the reason you and the wagon crashed."

Rona fell into silence, and Torregrossa figured that was just fine with him. They didn't have the time now to be debating this thing, especially with the only cover they had about to be sent hurtling down the mountain and with all those guns still on the loose.

"See anything?" Ethan called softly up to Danny as he worked his way farther under the wagon.

"Still clear, as far as I can see."

Ethan rolled all the way under, dropping into the hollow he'd fashioned near Rona. "Then give me a hand. Push when I tell you, and maybe this thing will roll."

Lying flat on his back, Ethan braced his feet against the edge of the wagon's side, took a deep breath, and started to exert pressure. "OK . . . now."

Danny was braced, shoulder pressed to the rough wood as he threw his weight, slight as it might be compared to that of Torregrossa, into the effort.

"Push!" Ethan called from below, keeping up his own effort,

trying to force his legs straight as Danny heaved and pulled against his end.

The damaged wood of the wagon creaked, and the reinforcing metal stripping groaned and grated as the freighter's weight shifted, beginning to yield to their combined strength and gravity itself. In slow motion, the wagon started to tip upright. Rona had time only to gasp once. Then, in accelerated motion, the wagon leaped upright, teetered an instant — allowing Danny time to release himself and jump back — rolled all the way over, and plunged downward, cartwheeling end over end along the mountainside in a series of disintegrating crashes that scattered pieces of the wagon in its descent to the bottom. The roar was thunderous, and the dust rose again in a swirling cloud. Gunshots were cracking in sharp counterpoint above them.

"Jesus," Danny muttered anxiously, looking around in amazement.

"That should bring 'em running," Ethan said shortly, rolling to his knees. "We've got to move." He met Rona's pained and apprehensive glance. "Can you?"

Rona tried, then shook her head in frustration. "My legs're still numb. I'm afraid all this work was for nothing. You're going to have to leave me."

"In a pig's eye." Torregrossa wiped his grimy shirt sleeve across his sweat-streaked forehead, thinking. Then he quickly ran his hands over Rona's legs. Nothing was broken as far as he could tell. "All right. You're going to have to hang onto me."

"What? How?"

He directed her arms, one up over his right shoulder, the other under his left arm to where she could interlace her fingers across his chest. An attempt to stand upright with the additional weight on his back at this precarious angle would have pulled him over backwards, so he didn't try. Instead, he remained on all fours and struck out for the freight road above them.

Danny scrambled ahead, keeping his rifle clear of the dusty ground, and a wary eye on the ledge that protruded above the road. He had thought himself ready for almost anything until he heard Rona's happy exclamation.

"Ty!" Rona burst out in happy recognition. "You were wrong about him, Ethan. He must have run Sam Reo off, or killed him."

Ethan and Danny glanced up sharply at Rona's exclamation and had just enough time to roll for cover before the lead came flying in their direction.

Chapter Seventeen

Sam Reo had been out-gunned and, for the moment, out-ma-neuvered, but that didn't mean he was going to give up. Not now. Harding might have caught him by surprise and run him off like a whipped pup, but Reo had more sand than that, and he prided himself on being more tenacious than a badger. Now that he'd sunk his teeth in, he wasn't about to let go.

He'd peppered the torn-out slash down the mountain before he had realized he was shooting at Rona Burr and her crew. He regretted that mistake, but had no intention of letting it slow him down in his pursuit of Harding. Besides, the end of Harding might mark the end of Rona Burr's problems . . . if she were still alive.

Reo leaned up against the cold, rough surface of the boulder where he had gone to ground, nursing a graze one of the men with Harding had managed to inflict on him before he'd taken stock of the layout. It wasn't bad — a bullet had torn a chunk of flesh out of his left arm, near the shoulder. It bled heavily, but that was the extent of the damage as far as he could tell. Still, he winced as he knotted the bandanna tightly around the wounded arm, with his free hand stanching the warm, sticky flow of blood. His horse was over the next ridge, out of sight, and he was sure undiscovered by the fools who had come after him. For the moment, he was better off on foot. He leaned his head back, the wall of rock bumping his hat forward to shade his eyes. He breathed deeply of the rarefied mountain air, sipping it like a cooling nectar, cradled his rifle in the crook of his arm, and gave thought to his next move. *Tyler Harding wasn't going to get down off this mountain alive, and it didn't matter what it would take to accomplish it.*

Tyler Harding stood on a broad, rocky ledge. He held a rifle in his hands and stared down the slashed and gouged mountainside. He had sent his men after Reo. That damned interloper wasn't going to get off this mountain alive. Not after this. Harding's next move was to take care of any witnesses — especially witnesses like Ethan Torregrossa who could haunt him for the remainder of his days. And, with a man like Torregrossa, those days could well be severely limited if Harding ever let his guard down.

His thoughts ran to Rona's hatred of Sam Reo, and he half smiled. His round face even took on a boyish, mischievous look. He raised his rifle above his head and waved it eagerly, silhouetting himself on the outcropping — the very image of a proud, conquering hero.

"His arm appears to have improved some," commented Torregrossa.

"What are you talking about?" Rona asked.

"Hey! Rona," Harding's voice called out, interrupting the conversation below. "Are you all right down there? Me and the boys I brought along ran Reo off!"

"Yes, I'm fine!" Rona called back. "We're fine! Tell your men to hold their fire. We're coming up."

Danny appeared startled by that plan and looked at Ethan. "We are?"

"Looks that way."

"Of course, we are," Rona insisted. "Ty wouldn't be up there in the open if Reo was still around. I wonder who he brought with him."

"So do I," Danny growled softly.

Torregrossa looked from Danny to Rona and shook his head. "Reo took off, far as I can tell. I figure that means he doesn't have any men with him. A man like that has to be outgunned before he'll let go. Have you given any thought as to why Harding would have collected some men and come up here armed to the teeth? Especially with his shoulder injured the way it was, arm in a sling and all?"

"What are you talking about? Look, his shoulder is fine. Are you still saying . . . that Tyler is involved in what happened?"

"Yes."

"That's ridiculous! Can we go up there, please? Will you help me, or do I have to crawl?"

Ethan cast a wary eye upslope. "All right. Let's go."

With Rona's arm around his neck, Torregrossa eased her up. This was one trip he wasn't going to make on his knees. He edged from cover, digging his feet into the dirt and pushing himself and the woman upward. Danny cussed, but he moved out, cutting off to the left, allowing the rifles above something less than the satisfaction of clustered targets.

Harding was the man to be reckoned with, not Reo. Ethan was a man to read the signs, and he felt that much in his gut. And here they were, easing up the slope in the direct line of danger. Sweat broke out across the back of his neck, and the tiny hairs along it prickled a warning. Carrying the full weight of Rona, he allowed himself to slide a little, giving the impression of faltering on the bad footing, slowing his pace.

"You reckon you can reach the horses?" Ethan directed the question at Danny as they paused, scattered out on the steep grade, catching their breath.

Danny grinned and nodded, stringy, brown hair flopping about his shoulders. "Sure can."

Rona grimaced. "Whatever are you talking about? Of course, we can reach the horses. It doesn't matter where you left them. Ty will cover us until we reach them. He might have even found your horses by now."

"Hope not."

Ethan's mind was racing. Reo was after Harding, or the other way around. It didn't matter which was which. The three of them were in the middle. Both Reo and Harding had arrived in Stillwater at about the same time. Since Sam Reo had come in the wake of Tyler Harding, Torregrossa had to guess it was Sam Reo who was doing the pursuing. Maybe Reo represented the law. In that case, he, Rona, and Danny had misjudged the situation.

Ethan had kept close to the towering pines not felled by the freight wagon's passage, keeping them just to his right. He wasn't as sure as Danny about the boy's chances of reaching the horses, but he did know it would only take one good stride, once he reached the freight road, to take him out of Harding's range of fire. And they had to have the horses if they were to stand a chance of getting out of their predicament with their hides whole.

"All right," Ethan spoke to Danny in a conversational tone, confident the words would not carry clearly to Harding above. He took a deep breath. "Start moving, Danny. I'll try to draw his fire off you."

"What?" Rona gasped as she struggled to be free of Ethan, trying to jerk one arm free from his grasp where he held her close to lift her up the hillside. Her feet sought purchase, but her legs were useless, buckling immediately, nearly dragging them both down the scarred earth.

Danny anticipated Ethan and dived to the left, scrabbling in among some low brush and rocks on the far side of the wide swath cut by the heavy freight wagon's earlier descent.

Instantly Ty's gun cracked from above, the bullets tracing a pattern in Danny's path. Ethan didn't wait for more. He toppled to the right, rolling and dragging Rona along with him into the pines. When they stopped, she was panting, her face pinched and white.

"Tyler . . . my God, what's he trying to do?"

She lay on her belly, her hand clinging to the earth to lock her in position against slipping farther down the slope. Then she twisted back around to face the road, worming up a few feet while peering up at the man she had trusted only a few moments before, the man with a rifle now pointed in her direction.

"He saw us, didn't he?" she asked. "He knew it was us."

Ethan put a restraining hand on her shoulder and held her close to the ground beside him. "He knows all right."

For a moment Rona's face was a blank. It was hard to accept the complete turnaround confronting her. Her stomach sank. *How can it be that a man I have considered a friend, even a protector, can shoot a gun in my direction? How could I have been so blind?* Thoughts raced through her head. *If Ethan is right, and it's Harding who is causing the trouble for the Burr Line, and not Sam Reo, then . . . ?* She didn't want to finish that thought, but she had to. *Then Harding is responsible for Hank's death.* The realization brought a painful tightness to her throat. She wanted to cry out, could feel the impulse in the pressure in her chest, but she wouldn't succumb, not now.

"Your legs appear to be all right," Ethan stated, halting the progressive darkening of her thoughts and motioning with his head in the direction of her legs.

Rona leaned back so that she could glance down. Unconsciously she had braced her legs beneath her. An odd, tingling feeling prickled up and down the length of each leg. And

148

they were beginning to hurt.

With a wan smile she looked at Ethan. "You're right, finally there's something to be grateful for. Even if it means more pain."

Ethan sympathized, only able to imagine what she must be feeling, learning that Harding may never have been on her side. He shifted his gaze, his eyes sweeping first past the area where Danny had gone to cover and then on to where Harding was perched upon the rock ledge like a vulture. Pondering the situation, Ethan wondered if he dared to leave Rona alone, even for a short while. It was then that Danny jumped up and made a wild dash for the road above. The kid was fleet afoot, but, almost the instant he had come up out of the brush, Harding's rifle started to crack from above.

Rona, half hidden behind Ethan, spotted Danny over the other's shoulder. She caught her breath as the boy lunged upward, surrounded by a hail of lead kicking up the dirt around him as he ran.

Ethan figured Danny to be home free as he watched him reach out for the road, now only a couple of feet above him in spite of the bullets snapping around him like maddened bees, and then the boy fell. It was so abrupt that it took an instant for cognizance of what had happened to sink in. Danny had dropped like a sack of grain and lay sprawled where the mountainside dropped off from the road, his rifle still gripped tightly in his clenched fist, the other arm dropped half across the rock-strewn edge of the road. He did not stir. The silence that followed was as profound as death itself. Ethan ground his teeth, aware that his stomach was wrenching forcibly inside him as a gorge rose in his throat.

"Oh my God," Rona whispered beside him, her eyes bright and glassy, brimming with tears. "We have to do something. He's alive, isn't he?"

Ethan nodded, thoughts careening around in his head. He had to get to Danny. Rona was right. They had to do something. The boy was so small to take a bullet. He clenched his jaw and grated out the words, forgetting entirely that Rona's legs had suffered some sort of injury. "I'm going after him. If I make it, the horses are just up around the bend. Cut through the trees and meet me there. If I don't, you take off out of here the best you can, keep to the trees, and try to reach that old miner you were hauling the load for."

Rona nodded in silence, now muted by shock, never taking her eyes from the place where Danny lay.

Chapter Eighteen

Ethan was squatting behind the protection of a huge pine tree's trunk, ready to propel himself forward. He intended to follow the desperate path Danny had taken, when Rona touched his arm, staying his uphill lunge.

"Look," she pointed in the direction of the boy.

Danny's foot moved almost imperceptibly, gaining leverage on the slope, and the one hand without a weapon was plainly braced against dirt and rock. In the next instant, he sprang to his feet, bent double, and ran like a madman. He was locked in a race that ended in a headlong dive that took him across the width of the freight road to sprawl at the fetlocks of their horses, standing ground tied beneath the rock ledge. The animals were nervous, but they had been well trained, and had moved only a few yards from where they had been when the shooting had started. In another moment, Danny had regained his feet. Then, giving Ethan and Rona a victory wave with his rifle, he turned, vaulting into the saddle.

The tight knot straining at the inside of Ethan's chest dissolved rapidly. *Fool kid!* If Danny were standing beside him now, he was undecided as to whether he would congratulate the cocky, self-important youth on his strategy, or give in to the deep-seated impulse that possessed him to kick the stuffing out of the kid.

"Let's get moving," Ethan ordered, his throat dry and tight as he slipped an arm about Rona's shoulders and helped her up. "We'll have to cover ground fast to meet up with Danny, and it won't take long for those men up there to figure out we're trying to give them the slip."

The feeling in Rona's legs had returned, but she was still unsteady on her feet.

"Hold on to me," Ethan said shortly, and snapped his six-gun up to send a few wild shots through the trees toward the road above.

Rona did as she was told and hung on, the acrid smell of gun powder filling her nostrils, the brittle crack of the Colt pounding away at her ears. Ethan shifted his arm around her to support her weight, and they cut diagonally across the incline, working upward toward the crook in the road where Danny should be holding the horses. He knew, until they met up with him, Danny would be in the safest position. All he had to do was keep himself and the horses close up against the sheer rock wall along the left side of the freight road, and, if he did so, it would be impossible for Harding or his men to shoot at him accurately.

Ethan kept a strong, steady pace while holding up Rona. His breath began to come hard. "I don't think they can see Danny from above."

"I hope you're right," Rona gasped back.

Gunshots popped in answer to his own brief volley, as Ethan and Rona were threading their way rapidly through the trees, but none of the bullets even came close.

"How far is it up to that mine you were hauling the timbers to?" Ethan asked as the terrain forced them to slow their pace and pick their way along.

"Couple of miles, maybe less, but it's a dead end up there. We better head back for town."

"Does Harding know it's a dead end?" Ethan asked, afraid he already knew the answer.

"Yes," Rona acknowledged, then sighed. "He'll block the road, won't he?"

Ethan nodded. "Most likely. Wouldn't you?"

Blessed silence had descended upon the mountain, gunshots stilled for the moment, but a life filled with hard living told Ethan that Harding would be on the move. By now the man must have figured he and Rona were moving on. Harding belonged to a breed of men Ethan knew well. Because of that, Torregrossa could predict Harding would have given up the rocky ledge the moment he discovered it was no longer a strategic position. He'd be coming after them. The dual-faced back-stabber knew the country as well as Rona. Ethan knew it not at all. That knowledge was one of many unsettling facts with which he had to contend once he eased Rona to the ground a couple of yards below the road.

"What are you doing?"

"I'm going to check up ahead. Danny should be nearby on the road with the horses."

Rona struggled to stand on the precipitous mountainside. "Take me with you."

Ethan shook his head. "It's too risky. If Harding and his men have found a way down and have found a spot from where they can get off a clear shot, I might have to move fast."

"There isn't any such spot up there. It's nothing but sheer rock."

"Then I won't have any trouble, will I?"

Ethan went on ahead, clinging to the side of the mountain in an almost perpendicular climb. He came through the trees, topping out with his head level with the road.

Danny was there, sitting his horse and holding the reins of Ethan's as he twisted nervously in the saddle to look behind him. His gaze followed along the edge of the road for some sign of his friend and the woman. He gave a tight grin when Ethan showed himself.

After one quick look around, Ethan disappeared, reappearing a few moments later with Rona. He helped her into his horse's saddle and handed her the reins. She expected him to swing up behind her. He didn't but gave a worried look instead.

"You gonna be able to sit a horse?" he asked, standing in the dusty road beside her, his heart pumping in an erratic tattoo.

"I'm all right."

Ethan gave a curt nod. "Good."

He wet his lips, half turning to Danny. "Take Rona up to that mine. Tell the miner what kind of a hornet's nest we've stirred up and barricade yourselves. That miner will add one to our number. Now, you push those horses all the way, son. It's going to be tight."

Danny didn't like leaving his friend, and his face showed it, but he had found Ethan's judgment to be sound in the past, and he knew his partner had to have something in mind to send them off alone. Hawk did nothing without purpose.

Rona had little experience with the workings of Ethan Torregrossa's mind, and she looked down at him appalled, then shifted to dismount.

Ethan put up a restraining hand, superior strength keeping her where she was.

"Are you crazy?" she demanded. "You'll get yourself killed up here alone on foot. This is treacherous country, and you don't even know how many men are up there."

"I work alone. I can't have someone close by me to be worrying about. You'd be surprised what a man alone, on foot, can do."

Unconvinced, Rona shook her head. "You're not what

I expected, based on what Hank had to say about you. And Ty . . ." — she broke off helplessly — "Ty Harding is my worst nightmare. Everything's all turned around. If you're killed. . . ."

"I'm sorry, Rona," Ethan broke in, "but I won't be killed, and I don't have time to argue with you."

He raised his hand, and in its descent gave the horse a sharp slap on the rump. The horse bolted, and Danny sent his mount along right beside Rona as if he had anticipated the movement of Ethan's hand.

"Damn it, Torregrossa!" Rona cursed as her hands became busy with the reins, fighting for control of the startled animal.

By the time she got the horse under control, slowed, and turned to look down the road behind her, Ethan had melted back into the sheltering trees and sparse brush. There was no sign of him. Nothing to tell her which direction he had taken.

"He usually knows what he's doing," Danny volunteered in an attempt to reassure her while they sat astride nervous horses. "We better keep moving."

"Well, he sure fixed it so we couldn't do anything else, didn't he?"

Rona was boiling, and she touched her heels to Ethan's horse without another word, sending him up the road at a dead run.

Danny followed. He didn't have to worry now that they wouldn't follow Ethan's order to push up to the miner's place, since Rona seemed to be in a mighty big hurry. The horses lathered up fast at the pace Rona set, and she was forced to ease back or risk having the animals drop from under them.

Danny stayed with her, all the while thinking about Torregrossa back there, alone. Thinking about the man's disadvantage with only one good eye. Thinking about how much they all had to lose. "I don't think Ethan ever trusted Harding

155

from the first time he saw him, though I can't say I know why he didn't," Danny said, once they slowed their pounding pace.

"And what about you? Was I the only fool to be deceived by that man?"

"Naw. I kind of figured him to be old and slowed down some."

Danny realized he had been seeing the man through the eyes of his own youth, seeing Ty Harding exactly the way the man had wanted to be seen. In fact, he was about the age of Ethan, and he'd sure moved fast enough when he'd been lining Danny up in his sights and pulling that trigger. Danny had no illusions. He had come close to not making it. Bullets had filled the air, and, if he had not dropped like a rag doll when he had, he was sure the next slug would have torn home and most likely he would be dead. It was because of Ethan Torregrossa that he had almost gotten himself killed, and it was equally because of him that he had remained alive.

"You trust him, don't you?" Rona said to Danny. "You trust him with everything."

Danny nodded, looking away from her. "Yeah, I do."

"But he's a gunman."

That jerked Danny's head back so he could stare at her. "That's all you figure him for?"

"I don't know him, Danny. That's what my brother told me . . . that he had hired a gunman."

The kid gave that some thought as they pressed on. Ethan had a quiet, subtle way of imparting knowledge and experience without seeming to be making an effort in doing so. Danny's style of learning had been much the same. When his partner spoke, he listened. When Ethan moved, he was right there beside him. Until now. Separated, Ethan would be depending on him to take care of Rona as well as himself. If anything

156

went wrong, Danny figured it would be his failure, not Ethan's.

"Then take it from me," Danny said gruffly, "he's just about the best man I've ever known. Far as I'm concerned, there's never been a man like him, never will be one again. If only one of us gets back to Stillwater alive, he's figurin' it'll be you. That's his plan, an' I'll see it through."

"I don't want anyone else dying for me," Rona protested. "Enough has happened already. It hurts too much, Danny."

"We're gonna make it. So's Ethan."

He wasn't lying. That was what he believed. If Ethan didn't make it, it would only be for one reason — that he had put himself in a position from which there was no turning back, no escape. And he would do that only to protect them. Danny was determined not to let such a situation arise. From the beginning, Ethan had stepped into the rôle of the father Danny had never known. It had happened quickly and as naturally as drawing the next breath. He hadn't thought about it before, but he had done a lot of growing up since. It was strange, a man like Torregrossa having taken on a green kid, one he'd almost gotten himself killed over. It had been as if both of them had realized from the very beginning that it was something that was not to be questioned, merely accepted. Now, Ethan had sent him on, prohibiting him from covering his blind side.

The horses were lathered and blowing from the run when they reached the miner's cabin. Danny was certain Harding and his men couldn't have made it to the cabin ahead of them, not with Ethan back there, but he slowed his horse, cut in front of Rona, and held his rifle at the ready. The kid was still a little green, but experience was aging him quickly. He eased up on the place with a learned caution, Rona close behind him.

157

"Karl? Karl where are you?" she called.

Almost immediately the massive slab of a front door of the stout cabin swung open, and a man, once tall and strapping, now older and a little bent by time, stepped onto the timber-braced porch. He ran a hand through a shock of straight, white hair and regarded the two on horseback from piercing, brown eyes, then bobbed his head enthusiastically in their direction.

"Why I'll be dipped!" He rubbed his chin whiskers, staring up at Rona, then giving Danny a glance. "Rona Burr! What in tarnation are you doing up here? You didn't ferget nothing in the last order I sent ye."

Rona frowned. "I was hauling up the timbers you ordered . . . in the note you sent me."

Karl Schmidt let his head sway slowly from side to side. "I didn't send to town for no new timbers. Why what would I need 'em for? This ol' mine gives me all I need to make a living. Now, why would I need timbers? I ain't adding any new shafts."

"Oh, Karl," Rona said, feeling sorry for herself for having been so stupid. "I'm sorry. We've brought you a lot of trouble."

The grizzled miner glanced sharply down the road they had just come up. "Trouble's my middle name. I've seen more of it in my time than water flowing in a creek." He cast his eyes quickly from Rona to Danny. "He's a good 'un?"

Rona couldn't help smiling. "Yes."

"All right, then. You've been ridin' them horses pretty hard, so I reckon what spooked you must be right behind you. Now, let's get them horses under cover, and you come inside an' tell me what's coming down the trail after you."

Danny grinned and nodded. He wasn't looking at the old man in quite the same way. According to Rona, this old-timer had lived in these hills the better part of his life. That was

158

quite a spell to get the lay of the land. If he was bound to help, they had just gained an edge.

Rona slid off her horse into Karl's arms, giving him an affectionate hug before dashing into the cabin, while he and Danny saw to the horses.

The cabin was as it always was. There was a feeling of scattered disarray about the place, but all of the eating utensils were clean. The curtains she had put up years before, though tattered and yellowed, still hung at the windows. The curtains were the only softening, feminine touch in the place. Karl had allowed her to hang them just to humor her. He wasn't much for the trimmings. A table and some straight-back chairs occupied the side of the room with a window while a rope cot stood in the opposite corner against the wall. The space close beside the stone fireplace was taken up by a rigid, high-backed bench. Rona had been making herself at home in Karl's cabin almost as long as she could remember. The first time was with her father. He had brought up a load of supplies when she was eight. With a twinge she realized she had not visited Karl since her brother's death, although the old miner had come down out of his beloved hills — as he called the towering cliffs and sheer drops — to attend the funeral in Stillwater. With deft, experienced movements, Rona put some fresh coffee on the stove, replacing the puddle of murky mud that had sloshed in the bottom of the heavy, old, cast-iron pot when she had lifted it.

When the door swung open behind her, and Danny and Karl spilled into the small room, Rona jumped.

"Well, hell, Rona," Karl scolded as he came through the door, "didn't I tell you to sell the line and start over somewhere else after your brother died? I thought you'd cleared out of this territory months ago."

"Without saying good bye?"

"When there ain't time, there ain't time," Karl grumped. "I'd rather think of you as alive than draggin' yourself up this here mountainside with killers on your tail. You should've gone."

"I just couldn't give in," Rona told him with a half smile. She sat down on one of the chairs beside the rough table and flinched at the feel of the sore and tender bruises running from her hips down the length of her legs.

Sitting down opposite her, Karl glanced from Rona to Danny. "So, what's this trouble you've hauled up here to me, an' what're you planning to do about it?"

"I lost the freight team and wagon in a rock slide a couple of miles from here," Rona told him.

"Heard something down the trail. Somebody try to do you like they did your brother?"

Rona nodded. "I should have seen it coming," she admitted.

"Not likely. You all right?" Karl's seamed face creased even deeper with concern.

"Yeah. Just a little battered and bruised," Rona assured him. "Danny, here, and his friend, Ethan Torregrossa, pulled me out. But what hurt more than anything was finding out that Ty Harding is as much, or maybe even more, to blame than Sam Reo for what's been happening."

"Harding?" Karl frowned. "Your pa called him a friend. You told me when Hank died. . . ."

"I know what I told you, but I was wrong." Rona blinked back the tears. "And now" — she sighed — "we have a real friend up in the hills somewhere on foot, trying to corner Ty before he can do any more damage. He wants us to stay here, with you, and wait for him. All I want," she said earnestly, "is for all of us to get out of this alive. I don't care about the Burr Line any more. I don't care about Sam Reo or Ty

160

Harding. I just don't want anyone else to die because of me."

"Hawk ain't gonna die," Danny interjected, and, looking at Karl, he explained: "That's Ethan . . . ? See he didn't know his name . . . ? Ah, never mind that for now. Point is, Ethan can take care of himself better than any man alive. An' he ain't gonna do no backing down."

Karl grunted in satisfaction, then took his shotgun off the wall pegs. "Well, if this friend of yours makes it, we'll be here, waiting." Karl made the simple statement of fact as he rammed a shotgun shell in each chamber.

Chapter Nineteen

Within a few seconds Ethan was clear of the receding riders. He'd made himself scarce by sliding back over the edge of the road and into the trees, growing in thick stands along the steep hillside. A damned good thing he'd done it, too. That crazy woman would have turned around and come back. He shook his head. Crazy magnificent, that was what she was. There were times when she thought of herself as weak. He could see the doubt in her at times. She'd said as much. But there was nothing weak about Rona Burr, or hesitant. She was the rare breed of woman this country couldn't chew up and spit out. She'd been hurt. More than once. Physically, mentally, and in her heart, but even though she got knocked down, she always got back up.

He skirted the road, keeping well within the protection of the trees, his head filled with thoughts of Rona Burr. Thoughts that he couldn't afford right now as his mind sought out a strategy to get them all off this mountain alive. As soon as he was sure she and Danny were definitely headed for the cabin, that Rona hadn't turned back and plotted to intercept him, he hauled himself up again on the one level piece of real estate in these parts, the freight road. He rolled on his belly in the dust, cursing at the jab of sharp rocks, gained his feet, and then stared up at the almost perpendicular wall of earth rising on the west side of the road.

It was time for Tyler Harding to find out a little something about the true nature of Ethan Torregrossa. He wasn't about to let a snake like Harding breathe down his neck or pepper his heels with lead. He meant to find a way up to take the fight to Harding, but on his own terms.

Trotting down the road in Danny's and Rona's wake, Ethan kept his eye glued on each passing foot of the sheer wall running alongside his course, until he spotted what he was looking for. A deep gouge cut in the hard-packed soil that ran from the plateau above down to the old freight road. A well-worn water course, a place where water that fell with torrential force on the plateau above sought the lower elevations by reason of its own weight and plunged down the face of the wall and beyond, continuing down the mountainside. Over the years, the trench it had left in its passing had become as wide as a man and a couple of feet deep. Only its fanning out across the surface of the road had prevented the freight route from becoming impassable. The cut swung around close beside some imposing boulders jutting out of the scarred earth. Plenty of smaller rocks were exposed along the length of the water's course, and Ethan saw what appeared to be soft spots in the face of the earthen wall higher up. He didn't think he could find a more likely spot.

He glanced around once more, acutely aware of his blind side. Earlier there had not been time for him to think about such things. It had been action and reaction. But, now, nothing could be overlooked. Everything had to be taken into account, including his own disadvantage. The blurred vision of his left eye could be a deciding factor, if he did not allow for it. He hadn't realized how much he had come to depend on Danny's being there, being half his sight. Now he felt the vulnerability he had ignored since the shooting had taken clear sight from his left eye. He tested, carefully, the scope of vision available to him in his right eye. He trusted his aim, well practiced since

163

his dive from the river boat. It was the peripheral vision that worried him. Too much depended on not allowing himself to be blind sided. He took a deep breath and cocked his head. Far in the distance he could barely make out a ripple of voices. Some of the words were even clear to him. Sound would be his ally.

Ethan started to climb. He inched his way slowly upward, feeling like a fly on a wall, knowing in the back of his mind exactly just how exposed he was. If either Reo or Harding happened along, he could very easily be a dead man. Or would Sam Reo pull out his picket pin now? He rather doubted it. Reo would kill to attain his goal. He would do it coldly and without hesitation, whatever that goal was, but Ethan was working his way through things and came to the conclusion that it was unlikely the man would eliminate bystanders unless they happened to get in his way.

Left foot wedged between rock and soft soil, right hand groping for a handhold above him in the cleft, Ethan pondered the other piece of the puzzle — Tyler Harding. He'd settled in Stillwater under a guise of respectability, and was anything but that. He was covering something, and he had blood in his eye. Ethan's instincts about the man had been right from the beginning. He was a cold-blooded killer who had had reason to sheathe his claws a while, working for Rona's father. Whatever that reason, Ethan was damned sure it was somehow tied to Sam Reo. Plainly Harding had been trying to throw suspicion in the direction of Sam Reo when it came to the problems of the Burr Line. He had fueled Rona's hatred of Reo whenever he had had the opportunity. But what was behind Harding's hatred of Reo still remained a mystery.

Despite the coolness of the mountain air, Torregrossa was sweating when he dragged himself upward, closed his hand over a large rock, and kicked his boot toe against the side of the gouge he was scaling. Nothing. He hung suspended for a moment, one hand clutching the rock, one foot braced against a smaller stone, while he tried to sink his other booted foot deep enough in the dirt to get a solid purchase. His hand and other foothold were unyielding, but his boot bounced painfully off the stone's surface, and then the other foot gave way, leather boot-sole grating sand against rock, zipping him out into thin air. For an instant, he dangled by one hand, suspended almost three quarters of the way up the rugged wall, hanging by the strength of the fingers of one hand. The sweat, already a mist between his chest and shirt, issued forth in a fresh waterfall across his forehead, running in tiny rivulets down his temples and nose, dripping off his chin. Ethan's body swayed slightly at the end of his arm while he scrabbled for a better hold. Muscles stretched and strained. A tingling feeling of panicky warmth surged up and down the length of his tensed body, burning into his arms and shoulders with a vengeance. The right hand, gripping the rock, clenched a little tighter, his fingernails bending and breaking, as his feet tried repeatedly to find a soft spot or rock that would give him the leverage upward that he sought. Finally his left foot caught and held, braced against shifting soil and deeply buried rock. For a moment he paused, gasping, strained muscles aching and trembling at the demand placed upon them. Then he drew a cooling breath deep into his laboring chest and lunged upward, ignoring the searing warmth racing along tortured muscles as he propelled himself up the cut with both feet and hands. The precarious foothold gave way beneath the added pressure, but he had already cleared it, scrambling upward, when it lost its seat in eroded earth, the entire bracing dissolving into a cascade of loose dirt and pebbles.

A lifetime of experience in not looking back stood Ethan in good stead as he heaved and scuttled relentlessly toward his goal above. His right hand snagged a small, scrubby plant, growing within inches of the top, firmly rooted in soil and wrapped deeply, determinedly among the rocks. The bit of scrub brush did not give as Ethan grabbed its slender trunk and used it to haul himself over the lip to sprawl flat on his belly in the dirt.

He quickly surveyed the scene spread out before him. Nearly flat, there was nonetheless a bumpy roll to the land and lots of low scrub such as he'd used to drag himself up over the rocky lip of the surprising flat. A few trees, big pines like the ones growing below, were scattered near where the land took another dramatic turn toward the clouds. He had worked his way to what was little more than a ledge high above the freight road.

Ethan stayed put a few moments longer to evaluate his position and get his bearings. The cabin Danny and Rona had lit out for had to be northeast of him, and there was plenty of rough terrain between here and there. Tracking would be difficult, but not just for him. If anyone were trying to pick up on him, it wouldn't be easy. And, with some distance between himself and the road, his thread would be even more difficult to trace.

He looked around. For the moment, there was no one in sight. The throbbing and pounding of his effort to get this far calmed, and Ethan rolled to his feet, dirt clinging to his clothes. He gave himself a shake, and small clumps of dirt rained from him in a brief patter. No gunshots echoed on the air. He would have easily heard the sounds of gunfire had there been an exchange within a couple of miles of where he stood. The clear mountain air transmitted sound rather than muffling it. He was grateful his hearing had become even more acute since his vision had been cut in half.

He shook his head vigorously, still half believing if he shook hard enough, if he strained and forced it, his vision would clear of its own accord. In public, he went to great pains to prevent others from noticing the loss. However, he knew some people might suspect and others guess if they'd watched him closely in recent days, but none, save Danny, knew for sure the extent of his handicap. And it was to his advantage to keep it that way. While it did nothing to slow him down, the knowledge of such a loss could be used to an enemy's advantage. He could not risk his enemy gaining that knowledge and coming after him with a gun.

Ethan turned and, in a half crouch, started back toward the rock ledge above the road where Rona's wagon had gone over the side and they'd been bushwhacked. He'd be able to pick up a trail there, despite the terrain, because he was good, damned good. He would find enough to give himself direction.

He moved like a big cat, and he moved fast. It was with a twinge of something unidentifiable that he gave full realization to the fact that it was the first time since he and Danny had teamed up and he had taught the boy to shoot straight that they were up against it with neither having the other to back him up. The kid was well able to take care of himself. Of this, Ethan had no doubt. Danny had plenty of sand, and he thought quicker on his feet than any man he'd ever been up against. Yet, there remained the fact that his experience was limited by his youth.

Ethan pushed the momentary thought from his mind and got down to what he did best. Danny had always managed to hold up his end of things in the past. Baptism by fire on the stagecoach had honed the young man's skills. He'd get himself and Rona where they needed to go. Ethan knew he could depend on that. Trouble was, he admitted to himself as he made his way across smooth, flat rock, pine mats and coarse soil, he felt a part of his former self rising within him like some oppressed bile. He wasn't sure he liked it, but it did simplify matters. The cold, calculating side of his nature allowed for cool-headed planning and expert tracking of man, any man. Danny had no such inner resources to call upon when things got rough. Everything about the kid was right out in the open. He did not possess the icy blood that flowed in the veins of Ethan. And for that, Ethan was grateful. Once this was over, he wanted the boy to find himself a life, a good life.

For now he had only to worry that Danny might hesitate where he would not. The kid might stop to think while Ethan would act with deadly speed, violence coming swiftly as his second nature. Ethan knew well his own darker, colder side. He doubted if Danny had yet developed this side of his personality. His own had taken years to cultivate, flourish, and grow. One thing he was sure about in Danny: the kid was a survivor. After that stage ambush he would trust the boy at his back any time. He had the stuff to bull his way through. What was required might go against everything Danny wanted to believe about life, about folks, about himself, but he would do what he had to do. That was the mark of a true survivor. The mark of a man, not a boy, who had been taught some hard lessons earlier than most.

Sliding his six-gun from his holster, Ethan eased up a slight rise in the land, sinking lower, closer to the ground, and slowed down as he approached the vicinity of the ledge. The terrain had become more lumpy, pocked with hollows and dotted with oversize boulders that could easily conceal a man with their girth. He slipped behind one.

Someone was nearby. Ethan could feel it, though he could see neither man nor horse. The echo of silence hung heavily on the air, making his ears ache in their effort to hear. Not the song of a bird or the chirping of an insect broke the deadly quiet. Something, or someone, caused the small creatures of the plateau to keep their counsel. Ethan knew the signs. Birds and animals fell silent before man's advance much the same as they fell still before the threat of a stalking, hungry predator.

With the solid roughness of a boulder pressing up against his left side, Ethan hesitated, allowing his senses to reach out into the surrounding emptiness, touching the presence of another. There was someone else out there, and, whoever it was, he was very close. Every tingling nerve in Ethan also told him that whoever it might be was on the move. The half blind gunman knew in that instant that he had been located, his approach noted, and he, for the moment, was the hunted.

It was nothing new to Ethan. He'd been stalked before, and by better men than Tyler Harding. The plantation, his early home, had been his first learning ground. The key, he'd learned then at a very young age, was concentration. The ability nearly to project himself from one place to another. To feel what was carried on the wind, to analyze the faintest sound. To be able to gauge his adversary and the moves that one was likely to make. That necessitated attention that had to be focused and held, no matter what else assailed him from within or without. Now, he controlled his breathing, kept his disadvantaged side pressed against warm stone, and waited. A gentle afternoon breeze was a soft caress against his face. He would have sworn he could hear the sound of his own sweat breaking out across his temples.

An insect started its soft chirping some distance behind him. Ethan heard it and knew his back was safe, at least as long as he heard the soft, sporadic chirping. Up ahead a bird fluttered down into some low brush and perched there, unruffled. He glanced in the direction of the small, feathered creature, then shifted his eyes from one side to another, probing, questioning. His hand, dry and steady, gripped the butt of his six-gun, shifting the muzzle in steady alignment with the direction he was looking.

Then, abruptly, hoofbeats pounded down the old freight road below, the sound bursting through Ethan's concentration like an explosion ripping through loose shale. Reflex took over. Ethan spun toward the road, away from the protection of the rocks, dropping flat to his belly so he could peer anxiously over the edge of the plateau, his attention focused on the thunder of the riders. There were three of them. Their horses were running full out, heading up the road, and all that lay in that direction was the cabin Rona and Danny had lit out for. At the head of those riders, slapping spurs to his mount, rode Tyler Harding, hunched in the saddle, a look of determination draped about him like a cloak.

Dust billowed up in a thin cloud, streaming from beneath the pounding hoofs of the horses below, and Ethan swore under his breath. Harding was the one he had expected to find up here, the one he was becoming more and more sure he had to stop. But that wasn't going to happen. Now all he could do was go after them.

Ethan was poised to rise. He had to make his way to the cabin on foot the best way he could, as fast as he could. Danny would have to hold them off, prevent Harding and his men from rushing the cabin until he could reach them. The kid could do it, and he had no choice but to depend upon that fact.

A boot scraped against rock. Ethan threw himself sideways, rolling over on his back, his six-gun swept up to cover the shape of a man standing just above him, holding an equally ugly weapon leveled at his gut.

Reo had managed to blind side him. Ethan had not caught the flash of movement from the corner of his eye that should have warned him of the other man's approach. He had only heard the footstep that had alerted him. Now he lay sprawled on his back, frozen in a grim posture of defense, feeling as vulnerable as an up-ended turtle, his weapon leveled at Sam Reo's belt buckle, the hammer pulled back.

Each man looked down the other's gun barrel with the undeniable certainty that both would be dead if either started the shooting.

"Mexican standoff," Reo muttered dryly. "You always take chances like that?"

Chapter Twenty

Sam Reo squatted down on his heels, real close, taking a big chance of his own. His gun, nearly in Ethan's face, never wavered.

Neither did Ethan's.

"You know, if one of us was to pull the trigger real fast, I don't reckon the other would have a chance to react, but then that'd be a damn' shame for us to kill each other or even to have one of us wind up dead when we both want the same thing." Reo made the observation with a smile on his dry, cracked lips. He rambled on a bit. "On the other hand, it's mighty interesting I was able to come up on a man with a reputation like yours the way I did."

Ethan ignored the whole thing, gun steady, eyes the color of steel on his adversary. "What the hell are you doing here, Reo?"

The other man shrugged at the question. "I was hoping to jump you and take your horse. Harding and his boys ran mine off a while ago. But it appears you ain't got one, either." He paused, his eyes still fixed on Ethan.

"Tyler Harding." Hawk muttered the name.

Reo's square features pinched a little in surprise. "You know?"

"You haven't pulled that trigger yet, so I'm guessing I was right that it's Harding behind the trouble the Burr Line's been having. You just did your share of keeping your mouth shut."

Sam Reo allowed the oily smile to slide from his face. "You're the smartest thing that Hank Burr ever did. Too bad he didn't get smarter sooner. Maybe he wouldn't be dead now." His stance relaxed just a bit. He rose, stepped back, then holstered his gun in an unspoken truce.

Ethan followed suit. The two of them squared off, facing each other, each still taking the other's measure.

"Exactly what do you want, Reo?"

"I've been after Tyler Harding for almost two years, although, until today, I didn't know it was Harding for sure. Almost had him a while back, but he slipped by me."

"You almost had me a while ago," Ethan reminded him. "My partner, too."

Sam chuckled softly, but the sound was like crunching glass and carried no mirth. "My mistake," he said by way of apology. "Nothing personal."

"I take it personal when someone shoots at me."

"You shot back."

"What's Harding wanted for?"

"Robbing banks and stages, killing more people than a poster has room to list. Bank tellers, stage drivers, a couple of women on the street in Waco. He ain't very particular. I've been trailing the son-of-a-bitch for nearly two years. Mind you, I didn't know it was Harding I was following, and I'll tell you I had damn' few leads. Harding changed his name at every turn. The trail ran out here, and I settled in. Well, as luck would have it, he hadn't come to rob a bank. I just waited, hoping that he would play his hand. But, you see, I'd never laid eyes on the man I was after. The description I had fit Tyler Harding, but there couldn't've been a mistake. I had to be sure, absolutely sure, it was him, 'cause, mister, I can't sleep until Tyler Harding is dead and buried deep in the earth." A fanatical gleam lit up the depths of Sam Reo's matte-gray eyes, igniting a spark of life there for the briefest moment before it was gone. "Now I'm positive. It took a lot of time. It hasn't been easy, having to sit back and let Harding try to ruin my name while he worked himself into a corner. But now I know, and now he's mine!"

"You going for the bounty?"

Reo took off his hat, slapped the dust from it against his leg, and resettled it at a cocky angle on his head. "Oh, yeah, I'll get the bounty, but that's not why that man can't hide anywhere on the face of this earth from me. He shot my younger brother, a banker, who was really gonna make something of himself. Didn't even kill him clean. Left him a pitiable cripple. I can't hardly look at him. Harding's gonna pay for that with his life, an' he's gonna do it the hard way. Then I'll collect on his hide. Ain't no doubt I'm goin' to take him in, slung over a saddle, and there's going to be little enough of him left to drag back. Ten thousand dollars for two years of my life and many more of my brother's."

"What about the life of Hank Burr?" Ethan spat the words with a bitter snap. "And the men working for the stageline?"

"None of my doing," Reo replied positively. "I told you Harding set all that up." He gave a wolfish, self-satisfied grin. "That son-of-a-bitch figured to get rid of me without winding up swinging from the end of a rope himself. He's known I've been on his coattails quite a spell. I spread the word whenever I moved from one town to the next. I wanted him to know I was coming after him. No matter how long it took." Reo shrugged. "It's too bad if the girl got killed, but she should have had more sense than to try and keep running the line alone. I tried to watch out for her, but I had my own concerns. You see, when the trail led here, and while I waited to be sure, I invested money for my brother. Full time care costs a lot, you know. Rona should have had sense enough to see through Harding. The man's scum."

Ethan seethed. Sam Reo wasn't a cold-blooded killer, but it was obvious that he was as single-minded. "Rona's not dead."

"Good for her." Reo responded to the revelation without enthusiasm and asked the next question because it was evidently expected of him. "She tore up bad?"

"No. She's all right. But she could have died under that wagon without help, and you would have let that happen, just as long as you could pin down Harding. I don't suppose it even occurred to you to go down and have a look, after the wagon went over the edge of the road?"

"I told you, it's Harding I'm after. Besides, how willing would Rona have been to accept any help from me. Hell, if I'd tried to help her, her first thought would have been that it was me who was responsible for the whole thing. Rona doesn't have any soft spot in her heart for me. Remember that when you want to give me advice. Anyway, how far would I have gotten if I'd've stopped along the way to pick up every person Harding trampled in his path? Stop him, and we'll stop all his killin' and hurtin'."

Reo gave Ethan a hard look. His eyes, mere slits beneath hooded lids, were empty. Ethan felt a chill in the pit of his belly. "You've grown cold, Reo. Rona needed your help these past months. You could have done more. You could have tried to convince her that you were on her side." Ethan paused. "How do you think your brother would feel about you now?"

"*You* were hired to look after her, weren't you?" Reo inquired angrily. "You do *your* job, and I'll do mine. And don't act so high and mighty. You're a gunman. Let's not talk about being cold. About my brother, Clay? Trust me, he

175

doesn't feel a damned thing . . . he's a vegetable."

Reo hit a nerve with his remarks, and Torregrossa locked eyes with the empty shell of a man before him and wondered, just for an instant, if his own eyes had ever seemed so devoid of life and emotion. If there had truly ever been a time when the only things holding his skin up from the inside were bitterness and hatred.

"We better both get to it, then," Ethan suggested. The hard planes of his face appeared chiseled from ice. He repressed his anger — this wasn't the time or the place. Yet, he felt it churning within him and finding no outlet. He wanted no part of this man whose private hell flowed so easily into other people's lives — yet, their goals were the same. And they could not risk falling over one another now.

"What's keepin' you?" Reo demanded abrasively.

"Guess you didn't notice, the man you're after just cut out of here, heading northeast, toward the end of the old freight road. According to Rona, the only thing up there is an old cabin and a miner. The way I see it, if Harding gets up there, and stumbles across Rona, I'll probably have to kill you to protect her. That's what I was hired for, remember?"

Reo's eyes gleamed. "Anything up at that cabin that'll keep him busy until we can cover those miles?"

"Rona and Danny and maybe the old miner, who counts himself her friend."

Ethan started to run as he tossed the words over his shoulder. There was no more time for talk. Reo was coming, or he wasn't. There was a risk, a big one, no matter which way it went.

Sam Reo was a relentless, patient man. Two years of his life had been spent on the trail of the man who now went by the handle of Tyler Harding, and he was not about to let him slip through his fingers. He had meant every word he'd said

176

to Torregrossa. The thieving snake was going to pay, and judgment day was at hand. Without another moment's hesitation, he took after Ethan at a pounding run in boots never intended for such punishment, sliding on small rocks and topping vegetation.

They were still a good distance from Karl's camp, blowing from their first run, walking fast, when Ethan and Sam heard the shots — several, spaced well apart, echoing separately on the clear mountain air. At the sound of the sharp reports Torregrossa picked up his stride again. He could only hope Harding and his boys hadn't taken them by surprise.

The gunfire pricked Reo into more speed as well, but his reasons were different than Ethan's. If the gunshots stopped, Reo knew it would be over, and his quarry would slip through his fingers again. He had ridden too many miles, spent too many nights on the trail, huddled close to a tiny, hidden campfire fending off the night chill, to allow his brother's assailant to catch him flat-footed again. Surprise today had permitted Harding to slip past him the first time on the plateau above the freight road. Reo had figured out quickly enough that Harding had set him up. He'd rigged the accident, and he had led Reo to it like a bull on the end of a ring in his nose. The bastard would have taken perverse delight in seeing Reo swing for a murder he himself committed. And it would've been easy to pin the rigged accident on Reo, to put himself forth as the injured party, and swear he had caught him at it, that he had tried to help Rona, but had been too late. Harding might have pulled it off, too. If Reo had been caught on that rock ledge when he had mistakenly drawn a bead on Torregrossa, he would have been finished. Instead, he had managed to worm his way past Harding and his men with skill and a tremendous amount of luck. The cost had been leaving his horse behind.

They were both laboring for breath when, traveling cross-country, Ethan and Sam spotted the place where the road began its gradual rise to meet the plateau. By the time the old miner's cabin came into sight the land had rolled together, leaving only a steep grade between the road and the plateau that spread out to include most of the miner's compound before it heaved up against some higher mountains jutting almost straight up behind the structure.

From the angle of their approach, Ethan spotted the cabin in the clearing just beyond a rim of trees, and to one side of the cabin he could see a huge, dark hole bored into the mountainside that could only be the mine opening. Both he and Reo dropped to the ground, sharing a fire in the lungs and a dryness of throat that precluded speech for long moments as they stared straight ahead and waited.

Ethan eased from his knees to his belly, drawing deep, sating breaths and getting a feel for the lay of the land, eyes sweeping slowly to and fro, seeking some sign of Harding or his men across the lumpy roll of the uneven ground.

"How many men were riding with Harding?" Ethan threw the question to Sam who lay sprawled on the hard earth beside him now, intently eyeing the same territory with similar intent. "Did I see all of them spread out on that road when they headed up here?"

"If you saw three of them besides Harding, then you saw all the dogs that run in that pack. At least, that's all I laid eyes on. Then, again, I was moving too fast to guarantee there wasn't another one tucked away somewhere. You can have the others. I want Harding, and I'm gonna get him this time." Reo paused, licked his lips, and pointed. "Look over there," he muttered softly. "Right over there's my ten thousand dollars on the hoof."

Following the direction of Reo's gaze, Ethan spotted a man stooped over by one of the corral posts on the far side of the cabin.

"You sure that's Harding?"

Reo nodded with certainty. "I'd know that skunk anywhere. I've been living with him in the same town for almost half a year. I ought to know the man when I see him."

Ethan's mind registered Reo's tone. He accepted the fact that Sam Reo would be of little use to him, at least willingly. Whether he could *make* use of him would be another matter altogether. He would have to guard against Reo's becoming a definite drawback. He could depend on Sam Reo for nothing more than the pursuit and killing of Tyler Harding, if it was within his power to do so. The man was so obsessed with that one idea he could well get himself killed and leave them short a gun on their side. Harding's boys were to be Ethan's business. Danny and maybe the old miner would perhaps lend help from inside the cabin. But, for the moment, those inside the cabin were unaware of his presence and would be making plans of their own. He would have to make his moves bearing that fact in mind.

Ethan's breathing had quieted considerably. He gave the problem his full consideration. It was a situation Ethan Torregrossa would have sworn, months ago, he would never have allowed to ensnare him. But cursing about it now wouldn't help. He was in it — he was up to his neck in it — and he couldn't walk away. He glanced sideways toward Reo whose face reminded him of a hound panting after its prey. Ethan was reluctant to ask anything of Sam Reo, but if Reo knew something he might be able to use, now was the time to find out.

"You got any ideas as to what Harding might be planning?"

179

Reo's eyes never left Harding when he answered. "He's slick. There isn't any way to tell which way he'll jump when he discovers he's about to be treed. But you don't need to worry about him. He's all mine. You go after the coyotes with him. I'll tangle with the wolf. He's all that I'm after. As soon as I nail Harding, I'm out of it."

Reo rose to a half crouch and began edging his way along the rise, looking for a better position in which to approach Harding. His softly spoken words of warning lay between them like stones.

Ethan's past experiences, the essence of his dark life, coiled up within him like a rattler. His eyes, narrowed and glinting, fixed on Reo as the man paused a few feet ahead of him. Then he bellied his way up the lip beside the vengeance-seeker.

In his faded, Southern drawl, soft and low, Torregrossa made his counterpart a promise. "I'm doin' what I have to do. If that includes stomping all over you to get where I'm goin', then that's what I'll do. I've got no stake in keeping you alive, Harding or no Harding. Keep out of my way."

The way Ethan saw it, Reo had been instrumental in creating this situation, whether he cared to take the blame or not. The man could sink or swim on his own. Meanwhile, Torregrossa hoped to all the saints that Danny, Rona, and her miner friend would be safe inside the cabin, the stoutest structure in the clearing.

"Fair enough," Reo grunted. "I'll keep that in mind." His thin lips separated and twisted into something bitterly resembling a grin. "You best remember what I said when the lead starts flyin'."

Feet beneath him, crouched and ready, eyes flicking over the clearing where the cabin occupied one side, Ethan expected to catch another sight of Harding and his men. It was best to have the enemy spotted before a man made his move. Reo

180

shifted next to him, his gun in his hand. It was quiet now. The sound of gunshots markedly absent.

Then Ethan saw why. Harding's two men were slipping along the blind side of the cabin. Each carried a flaming brand in one hand, a six-gun in the other. Their intent was to burn out the occupants of the cabin. It was no wonder. The cabin was built like a fort. Its only flaw was the blind side with no windows. At least, Ethan could now be certain that his friends were inside the cabin.

Hawk half rose. This wasn't the way he had wanted to play it, but he had no choice. He couldn't let them touch off that fire. He had one dead in his sights when the front door swung open abruptly. For an instant Danny stood framed in the doorway, only partially sheltered by the door, then the barrel of his rifle whipped around as he spun, spotting his targets, torches in hand. Behind him, Rona gave a startled yell when Danny's weapon roared as he levered the action with incredible speed, ejecting one shell and freeing another. In an eye blink one man was down, and the other was running toward a pile of rocks that was apparently waste from the mine. Danny's rifle kicked up a trail of lead following him the whole distance. The torches were left behind and lay sputtering in the dust until the flames shortened, dying back to nothing more than wisps of smoke curling up from charred stumps.

Reo shook his head, easing back on his own trigger for the moment, waiting for the volatile situation to settle down. A brittle smile of admiration sharpened the square angles of his dark face.

"That kid of yours is more than half crazy."

"He's not my kid . . . he's my partner."

Reo gestured toward the cabin. "Is that why he protects your blind side?" He said no more, but edged forward, his quarry in sight.

Ethan gave a start at Reo's remark. The man had seen the signs and figured it out. He stared at him a few moments, then shifted his gaze in the direction where he had last seen Harding as the action died down near the cabin. Danny's left side was exposed now to Harding, but Harding was unaware of Reo's approach as he belly-crawled toward the outlaw.

Ethan knew Harding wouldn't pass up the opportunity to take Danny out. He watched as Reo moved steadily forward, then he shifted his full attention on Harding who was visible again, and he decided Danny was far more important to him than giving a damn about what Sam Reo wanted. He snapped off three shots in rapid succession, the kick of the six-gun firm against the dryness of his palm. He dropped and rolled several feet, knowing his last location would draw fire in return. Reo, exposed by being half in the open, flattened in the dust with a vile curse while Torregrossa's bullets snapped overhead.

Startled by this sudden flank attack, Harding got off one shot that went wild, slamming into the door and splintering the wood beside Danny, before he dodged behind a thick, sheltering corral post. Harding, however, recovered quickly, hesitating only an instant behind the post before he turned and bolted toward the back of the cabin, out of Ethan's range.

Sam Reo came to his feet in a roll, every movement telegraphing pure fury when he threw a quick glance over his shoulder in Ethan's direction. Then he took off after Harding like a scalded cat in a running crouch.

On an upslope behind the cabin that was littered with old timbers and more rock waste, Ethan spotted Harding's remaining man. He took a couple of shots at him, but knew the range was bad for his hand gun. Still, a man could hope for a little luck.

Chapter Twenty-One

For an instant, Rona appeared in the doorway, intent on dragging Danny back inside the cabin. The kid stood his ground, the thick, wooden door acting as his shield. He glanced in startled recognition toward where the supporting gunfire had issued.

"That's gotta be Ethan," Danny called into the cabin as the scattered gunfire continued. "He got here quicker than I figured."

"Get back inside, or he's going to find you dead!" Rona exploded.

Torregrossa heard Rona's remark from where he sat behind the lip above the basin, and he couldn't help smiling. The little lady had spunk. He had to give her that. If he could just get her out of here alive, she'd do OK.

Danny pulled back, and the cabin door slammed shut with a thud loud enough to collapse a mine timber. How Danny had known about the attack on the cabin's blind side Ethan couldn't guess, but the moment the door slammed shut, Harding's man began a wary shift in his position. Another attack would come soon. And the next time Danny's instinct, or whatever had aroused him to the imminent danger, might not warn him soon enough.

Ethan hunkered down behind the ridge of earth and rock that separated him from the basin below, reloading his hand gun. If there were nothing more to consider, he could let Tyler

Harding and Sam Reo go off in a dark corner and kill each other like a pair of snarling, rabid, coyotes, but there was more involved. There were innocent people, good people, caught in the crossfire of their hatred. Yet, Harding was the key. Without him, the remaining man who had ridden with him would pack it up and pull out.

Torregrossa knew he had to go after Harding, Sam Reo be damned. He harbored no delusions. Harding would, without the slightest hesitation, blast into the next world anyone who stood in his way. The old Ethan Torregrossa was again present, but now there was a difference, one too large and cumbersome to overlook. In the past he had lived his life as one who was alone — cold, efficient, deadly. Now there were others to consider, and his old self, when it appeared, had its limitations when it included protecting others besides himself. Still that old self could be controlled, utilized, even turned to advantage, if he cared to make the effort. He would make the effort for the sake of the others, and he did owe a debt to Hank Burr.

Ethan's mind wandered to the time in the past when money governed his life. It had begun to become less a truth from the first day he had met Rona's brother. He had taken a job in a little town not much bigger than Stillwater. Wolf's Creek it had been called. The good people of the town had hired Ethan to make their streets fit to walk again. It had been a wild, god-forsaken place populated by ne'er-do-wells, pious idiots, and outlaws. And the folks who had considered themselves the good people had been willing to stand by and let him die because his methods had not wholly met with their approval. All but Hank Burr. He had been a stranger, passing through town, and he had backed him. Not because of any money he would receive, or thanks, or because he liked the strange, dark man. He had done it because Ethan had stood in the right. It hadn't mattered that Hank had known what

184

Ethan was. And it had been the young Burr's gun that had averted a blood bath that could only have ended in Ethan's death, alone on a dusty street. Well, not exactly alone. He had been planning on taking along with him as many of the outlaws as possible before he breathed his last breath.

When Hank Burr had stepped out from the crowd and aligned himself with Ethan Torregrossa on that broad expanse of dusty, open street, Ethan had thought the young man crazy. But if Hank had been crazy then, Ethan was the same kind of crazy now. And he had been crazy since the night the Cade brothers had sent him tumbling over the side of the paddle wheeler. That had been only a couple of days after he had left port in response to Hank's letter about his troubles in Stillwater that had included a bank draft for a couple of hundred dollars as a deposit on his services.

Hank had taken an accurate read of Ethan during their brief association. The money had started Ethan in Stillwater's direction. The debt he owed to the young man would have meant nothing to him. For most of his life he had not acknowledged debts. He had asked for nothing from anyone and expected the same. Hank Burr's foolhardy impulse to join him in the street had been his own lookout. Hank had recognized that.

Hank Burr had been intent on buying protection for his sister, Rona, and he had known what he could expect from the gunman. Torregrossa would root out the core of the trouble plaguing the Burr Line, and he would be able to pull the trigger when it became necessary. Hank had been no gunman, but he had been strong, honest, and willing to fight. Trouble was, he had found himself in water out of his depth. Nothing in his experience had prepared him for a Tyler Harding or a Sam Reo. Everything in Ethan's life had. And it was no wonder that Hank had gotten himself killed shortly after the

185

letter had been written. Even without the delays that had plagued Ethan, he would have been too late to do Hank any good.

Ethan slapped the last new round into his six-gun, flipped the loading gate closed, and edged over the lip of rolled earth. He shook his head once, clearing it of distracting thoughts. For the moment the cabin was quiet, and Ethan crept forward, keeping low, intent on slipping around in the opposite direction Harding and Reo had taken, determined to intercept them before more damage was done. His six-gun gripped tightly in his hand, he held himself in a tuck as he ran, keeping off the skyline and moving fast. He hadn't covered twenty-five yards when he froze, diving for the cover of the trees. He had spotted Harding slipping around behind the cabin, keeping wisely to the rocks and old piles of junk littering the area around the dwelling. Reo was still some distance behind, his posture and speed attesting to the fact that he had, at least for the moment, lost track of his prey. But he was like a hound on scent. He wasn't about to give up. Harding was now standing behind the blind side of the cabin, but Ethan's position didn't give him a clear shot at the man. Ethan swore silently to himself and waited.

He didn't have to wait long. Harding caught sight of Reo, closing the gap between them, even before Reo was aware of Harding, and opened up on him. Ethan watched the running gun battle closely and held his fire as the pair moved across the face of the mountain harboring the old mine. He could see the gaping hole of the mine's entrance still well above them.

He curled his lip. It wasn't his fight. Not so long as it didn't involve either Rona or Danny. If the rest of them got lucky, maybe the two on the mountainside would kill each other and end it. Torregrossa hesitated. He could see Harding's man. Without instructions from his leader, he wasn't sure of what to do. From what Ethan could see, he was doing his damnedest to catch a glimpse of what was going on. In the meantime, the gunfire picked up on the mountainside above the cabin and continued unabated as Harding and Reo took shots at each other.

Ethan was working his way among the trees ringing the cabin's clearing, trying to position himself in cover that would afford a fair view of the front of the small house, when he saw Reo flinch, fold up on the slope, and slide several yards before stopping himself in a skittering shower of dirt and pebbles. Seconds dragged. It appeared to Ethan that Reo was hit badly, but then Reo rose unsteadily to his feet. Ethan flicked his gaze once again in Harding's direction. He blinked at what he saw, startled. Nothing. Tyler Harding was nowhere in evidence. He had disappeared.

The man was as wily as a fox. Still, he could not have gotten far. Nor would he have wanted to, what with Reo still on his tail, closer than ever. That was a piece of business Ethan did not think likely that Harding would leave unfinished. Not when he had gone to such lengths, planning the freight wagon crash and luring Rona up here to be the victim, to ensure his own freedom. Even if he had seen Reo go down, he was too meticulous a planner to believe him to be dead without checking out the corpse. He was being cautious, and that was the mark of a reasonably sane man.

Long minutes passed in deadly silence. Nothing moved, and no gun was fired. Now Reo, too, was out of sight after scrambling downhill in a flurry of sliding tailings. But Ethan knew where he was. He had seen him take cover behind an old wagon with a broken axle, listing to one side at the base of the rock-strewn grade. They were both playing a waiting game, each waiting for the other to make the next move. The way Ethan figured, it was Harding's move. Ethan himself would have been more than willing to add a little spice to the situation if he could have drawn a bead on the murderous outlaw, but he couldn't shoot at what he couldn't see. Reo, for his part, did not seem inclined to make a move, so Torregrossa slipped up tight behind a tree also to wait. He was half tempted to shoot Reo and be done with it, but he knew all too well that Harding would not pull out now, even if Reo was dead. It was far too late. He would see all of them as unfinished business.

The leaden silence suddenly ended in a volley of gunfire, echoing from the blind side of the cabin. Ethan didn't like it. He wanted to move, but he knew how exposed he was, and Harding's man wasn't that far away. His eyes narrowed, and he licked his lips, cursing under his breath. He'd been careful to give away as little as possible. But so had Harding. Ethan still couldn't pinpoint his present location.

Rona's voice cried: "My God, they're going to burn us out."

Not having a clear view of the cabin's blind side and unable to see the pile of débris ablaze next to the wall, Ethan was caught off guard. All he could think was that Harding was going for broke at this point. He was bent on destroying them all as quickly and efficiently as he could. It was the desperate move of a man treading a fine line between hunted and hunter. But it would take a while for the cabin to begin to burn in earnest.

Now Ethan could see the smoke, rising from the flaming débris. An instant later, sunlight glinted off a gun barrel, catching Ethan's eyes from another direction. Harding's man was running in the direction of the cabin, a gun in one hand, a flaming brand in the other. The man lobbed the torch onto the cabin's roof, and sparks exploded across it. It was too late, but Ethan's gun kicked against his palm. It was hard and re-assuring, and the second of Harding's men jerked, then pitched forward to the ground, face first, arms flung wide.

The flames were beginning to take hold on the wall of the cabin at the same time the breeze began to pick up. Since Rona has cried out, not a sound or a movement had emanated from the cabin. Ethan was hoping it would remain that way for just a little longer when the door burst open and Danny emerged on the run, carrying a blanket.

The kid slapped at the spreading flames in an effort to smother them while Ethan tried to cover his partner. It was a fool stunt, but Danny had little choice. There hadn't been any rain in those parts for months, and the cabin, with all of its contents, would blaze hard once the flames took root. Their only other choice had been to run for it — all three of them, and one of them an old man. Danny had chosen the option Ethan should have expected. The kid was counting on him for cover, on Ethan and the old-timer in the cabin.

Danny beat back the crackling flames by inches, as Ethan shagged it from one tree to another, working his way toward the cabin. The flames at the wall of the cabin were nearly smothered when a bullet whanged off the thick bark near Ethan's head. Then, as if by magic, Tyler Harding materialized from the black opening of the mine. He was in clear sight for only a few seconds before he disappeared down into the tangle of brush and rocks behind the cabin. Ethan wondered if the cabin had a back entrance and figured a man living up here alone and mining had better have one. Dismissing the thought, Ethan snapped off a few shots, aiming them into the brush near where he had last seen Harding. There were no return shots. That was puzzling. Ethan momentarily directed his attention back to Danny who continued to smother the flames. The boy made a clear target. Why wasn't anybody trying to stop Danny? Then the question whether or not the cabin had a back door ran through Ethan's thoughts, and it dawned on him. *With Danny outside, Rona and the old miner were alone in the cabin. Of course, the cabin had a back door. Rona! There would be no better way to set Torregrossa and Reo against each other. The outlaw hadn't continued his assault on the cabin because he wanted Rona dead. No, it was just the opposite. Now he wanted her alive.*

Ethan understood. With Rona as a hostage, Harding would rid himself of either Reo or Ethan, maybe both, since it would only be a matter of time before they would be on each other like a pair of vicious animals — Reo wanting Harding, and Ethan wanting Rona. The tactic was almost flawless. But not if Ethan could stop him from attaining his goal. Harding was counting on the fact that Ethan would do anything in his power to protect Rona, and Reo would stop at nothing to get at Harding.

Ethan was off and running in a flash. Legs pumping, gun clenched in his hand, Ethan pounded across the hard-packed earth.

"Danny! The cabin!" Ethan shouted.

The kid wheeled, dropped the scorched and sodden blanket, then raced for the door. Ethan reached the shelter of the cabin and preceded Danny to the door. He hadn't spotted Sam Reo anywhere on the slope. Reo might have been hit worse than either Torregrossa or Harding had thought, but Ethan figured it more likely that Reo was lying back, waiting for his chance to take Harding down hard and for good.

Ethan slammed through the front door, Danny hot on his heels, not understanding his friend's anxiety, but snatching up his rifle from beside the door where he'd left it. The rifle cocked in his hands almost of its own volition, and Danny stood shoulder to shoulder with Ethan, feeling the silence, the emptiness of the cabin.

Outside, gunshots echoed briefly as Ethan spotted a crumpled form lying near the old stone fireplace. He squatted down beside the old man as now total quiet descended.

"He's alive," Ethan said softly. "He's bleedin' some, but it looks like Harding was in too much of a hurry to kill him."

"Harding?"

"Yep," Karl Schmidt roused himself enough to agree. "It was that sorry excuse of a bitch's whelp what took her. Damned sorry I am about it, too. He caught us by surprise."

Torregrossa glanced around the cabin. Signs of a scuffle were evident. There was a rear door, and it was open, swinging freely on its thick, leather hinges as a soft breeze blew down off the surrounding mountains.

"Only a few seconds," Ethan murmured, standing in the back doorway, reloading his gun and looking toward the slope thickly covered with brush. "She can't be far. We have to catch them before Reo takes on Harding again. We're gonna have to move fast."

Danny handed Karl some water from a bucket beside the hearth. "You'll be all right?"

"It'll take more'n a weasel like that one to slow down Karl Schmidt."

Danny joined his partner in the doorway, rifle at the ready, his gaze sweeping the same slope Ethan studied.

Karl collected his weapon from the floor, gained his feet, and half stumbled up to the pair of younger men, gingerly rubbing the back of his head, fingers coming away bloody.

"That 'un ain't gonna take himself far from a good horse," Karl observed.

"There!" Danny spoke over Karl's voice. "Look there." He pointed to a spot about halfway up to the mine where two figures were picking their way across the slope below it, skirting off to the left of the mine opening.

Directing his good eye to follow the direction Danny was pointing, Ethan spotted them. Then sweeping the slope to the right, he located Sam Reo, rising like an apparition out of the thick brush. For an instant the gun in Reo's grasp appeared oversize as he brought it to bear, swinging the barrel to center Harding in his sights. Reo didn't move quickly. Every shift, every movement telegraphed his intent. He was going to be absolutely sure this time. Harding was buzzard meat. Ethan wouldn't have given a damn about Harding — cold-blooded murder was a suitable end — but Rona was in the same line of fire. It would be a miracle if Reo could fire on Harding and avoid hitting Rona. And Sam Reo, Ethan was sure, counted Rona of such little importance that he wasn't even going to try to miss her.

Steadying his gun with both hands for the uphill shot, Torregrossa peppered the brush with his slugs. Reo started and pulled back under the barrage. Ethan had him pinned, unable to break cover long enough to get off a clean shot.

"By God, he'd a cut her in half to get to Harding!" Danny exploded.

"We've got to take out Harding if we expect to see Rona alive again," Ethan stated coldly. "If he slips past us now, he'll kill her sure as we're standing here. Or Reo will."

Danny slapped his rifle butt to his shoulder, lined up Harding in his sights, caught sight of Rona's lithe form, then shifted the weapon, and started laying down well laced shots in front of the outlaw. The kid knew his shooting was good, but he broke into a sweat out of fear of hitting her as his rifle bullets stitched a path across the hard ground and small puffs of dust rose from the earth close enough to clip Harding's boot toe. Harding pulled up short, paused only an instant in his stride, then turned and gave his captive a rough push toward the mouth of the mine.

Ethan and Danny cursed in the same breath, Karl joining in the chorus, before they all bolted out the door, climbing the gentle slope of tailings toward the mine opening, not one of them giving much thought to the threat of Sam Reo. At the mouth of the mine, Torregrossa and Danny stopped while they waited for Karl, pounding up anxiously behind them, a rifle clenched in his hand.

"There any cover inside?" Ethan threw the question over his shoulder to Karl in a raw whisper.

Karl shook his head. "Naw. There ain't nothin' left this close. I work much deeper in the mine where the ore hasn't played out yet. I cleaned it out good here. But. . . ." His words were not encouraging, and he appeared worried.

"Well?" Ethan prodded. "But what?"

"He wouldn't be stupid enough to take her deep into the mine. Even if he don't give a fig for her, he has to have a care for his own hide. There are a lot of shafts in there. Some're deep as a slide to hell. Got some of 'em covered with old timbering, but I don't reckon that's any too stable by now. I know my way around in there, but this fella and Rona don't. It'd be mighty easy for a body to step on the wrong thing and go down."

"Good." Reo's voice whipped out at them from above. "Maybe he'll do that and break his damned neck. Save us all a lot of trouble blasting him out of there."

Ethan glanced up to see Reo, standing braced with one boot digging sharply into the ground where the earth took a steep climb above the mine entrance. The left side of his shirt was splattered with blood, but the wound was not serious, or he could not be climbing around the rough, rocky terrain without being slowed to a crawl. The fact that he was here now meant he had been moving mighty fast.

193

A grim smirk lined Reo's face. "You've got yourself another gun. I'm goin' in with you," Reo announced firmly. "I wouldn't want anyone else bagging my prize. I'm even willing to forget, for now, that you took a few shots at me a while ago when I had Harding cold in my sights."

"I'm likely to do it again," Ethan told him. "And next time I won't aim to miss. It goes against my nature." His final words hung with ice.

Reo snorted. "Harding's a murderer, thief, and worse. I won't let you protect him, and I'm going to get him no matter what it takes."

"Yea! And I'll shoot you, if you hurt Rona doing it," Ethan shot back. "I'm not forgetting he's worth ten thousand dollars to you as well, so don't go giving any moral lectures about your right to vengeance. Remember this . . . you had it pegged right when you said it's my job to protect Rona. It is, and I'll do it, no matter what it takes."

"It's always the innocent ones who wind up dead because of a man like that," Reo persisted. "If I let him slip past to save Rona's life, it'll be someone else next week and someone else again next month."

"I'm not interested in your speeches," Ethan snarled. "Just remember what I told you."

"We better move," Danny said out of the corner of his mouth.

Ethan edged into the mine's interior, drew no fire, and ducked inside. Danny slid in alongside the opposite wall. Reo came in behind Ethan so close he could have been his shadow. Karl came in last, retrieving a couple of coal-oil lamps and torches from where they were stored inside the mouth of the mine. He handed one to each member of the party.

"He found my stash," Karl said. "Got himself a coal-oil lamp. This is my old girl, but she ain't none too secure. Sure

194

hope he knows something about mines."

"Don't know how, unless he robbed one," Reo suggested, holding his lit torch aloft. "Let's get moving."

The play of dark and shadow did unkind things to Sam Reo's face. It was lined, harsh, and bitter age showed as if it were a paper mask. Ethan raised his torch, holding it slightly ahead of him, and they started down the main shaft, following it quickly about seventy-five feet to where it forked and began a sharp descent into the mountainside. Reo examined the entrance of one passage while Ethan did the same with the other.

By the glow of his torch, Ethan spotted fresh scuffs and scratches in the hard floor, signs of one person struggling with another and being dragged forcibly down the right shaft. "This way," he said, and started down the shaft at a trot several paces ahead of the others.

Another fifty feet farther in the passageway another side tunnel intersected with the main shaft. Again they searched the floor and sides of the shaft for some sign to tell them which direction Harding had taken with his prisoner. Finally, in frustration, Ethan swore. At this point, the floor of the old shaft was too hard packed to give any indication of recent passage along its length.

"We're going to have to separate . . . ," Ethan started to say.

Karl interrupted: "Wait."

The old miner didn't hesitate to see if they heeded his words, but instead walked softly several paces down one passage, stood in silence, head cocked, then returned and repeated the action on the second fork of the shaft.

"This way," he informed them without the least doubt.

"You're sure?" Ethan asked him.

Karl nodded. "It's hard to explain, but I've worked this

mine for years, and other mines before this all of my life. It's a feeling, but I've seen few times when I wasn't right. A man works a mine, he gets so he can tell when there's someone in the passage ahead of him."

"All right," Ethan growled uneasily, swinging his torch in a broad arc from side to side, illuminating the walls of crumbling earth. "Let's go."

"Wait," Karl protested again, touching Ethan's arm.

"Wait for what, now, old man?" Reo demanded. "You said he's down there. I'm sick and tired of waiting, and I'm going in to get him."

Reo ignored the others and started, without caution, down the passage the old man had chosen. He moved at a slow run, his gun in one hand at the ready, the torch held high in the other so as to cast a puddle of light before him.

Anxious to be with the obsessed Reo when he reached Harding, but sensing urgency in the older man's voice, Ethan asked: "What is it, Karl?"

"That passage is a dead end," the old miner blurted. "There're some old, useless carts and tools down there, but not much else. It opens into a large chamber because that's where one of the original upright shafts was sunk. I ain't worked in there for years because the timbers and planking were rotten when I got the place, and the vein there was all played out. Almost anything could make the whole place go. A loud noise, a gunshot, anything."

Torregrossa cringed inwardly. He had never liked dark holes in the ground. They were little more than tombs waiting to happen. Up in the Appalachian country, he had seen the results of a cave-in where old timbers had given way. He had worked with the exhausted, dirt-encrusted miners from the outside, digging to free those trapped inside. It sent shivers of old memories shooting up his arms as a cool breath of air from the mine's interior kissed his cheek.

Reo was up ahead. They couldn't move with the caution that was advisable. They plunged into the shaft in Reo's wake, Danny glancing anxiously at the crossbeams overhead as they pressed on.

Chapter Twenty-Two

The sharp crack of two gunshots so close together they blended into one, echoing the length of the passageway until it reverberated with the sound, brought Ethan, Karl, and Danny to an abrupt halt just short of the large chamber Karl had described. To a man, they instinctively flattened themselves against opposite walls as the ricocheting whine died into silence.

From Ethan's position, he could see the inside of the chamber and the flickering glow of torch and lamp, but he couldn't spot either Harding or Rona. Nor could he see Sam Reo who had somehow slipped inside. Ethan leaned slightly forward. Light flickered against the wall and filled the chamber with surprising brightness. Reo had obviously gotten himself in close proximity to Harding and Rona. Another shot cracked sharply nearby, and Ethan jerked back against the cover of the sheltering wall.

Harding chuckled, the sound low and rolling, echoing hollowly within the confines of earth, rock, and rotting timbers. "Hey, Torregrossa!" he called out, the harsh sound of his voice and its reverberations giving Karl reason to shudder. "Wondered how long it would take you to get here. You say you care about the woman, but your friend, Reo, doesn't give a damn, and he came on a lot faster."

"You're a fool," Ethan snapped.

Again the rumbling chuckle. "You're right. But we have a

problem. Seems like, because of Reo, I'm in a corner I wasn't figurin' on. Hell, I'm willing to bargain. Let me through and the woman's yours."

Three shots exploded in rapid succession, the piercing whine of their ricochets screaming about the mine's cavity until ears ached and the air vibrated.

"You ain't going nowhere without goin' through me," Reo's voice sang out. "You're a dead man, Harding, or whatever your real name is, and it's my bullet that's going to put you to bed with a pick and shovel."

"It's up to you, gunslick. You get him off my back, or I'll throw this little wildcat down a very deep hole I found under some boards back here."

Ethan glanced sharply at Karl who nodded miserably. "Got to be the old shaft."

From the far side of the chamber, Harding emphasized what he said by brutally pushing Rona into sight, fingers wrapped tightly in the belt of her pants, holding her only inches from a large, square patch of wood lying over the dirt floor. It had at one time been a substantial seal over the unused shaft, but it no longer appeared very strong. Even from a distance the wood looked splintered and rotten. It wouldn't take much to send her plunging through it to the bottom of the shaft.

Rona didn't make a sound. She was scared. Her skin was ashen in the cold light cast by torch and lamp in the low-ceilinged chamber. Her lips were a thin, bloodless line, but the fire in her eyes burned brightly.

For the moment, Torregrossa was willing to go along with Harding's demands. The man could be found again later, in a place where they would settle the matter between just the two of them. That was, if Reo did not find him again first. It didn't matter which, once Rona was safe. Now, though, his only choice was to back down and get Rona clear of the shaft and out of the crumbling, old tunnels. Although it was risky to believe Harding, and bordered on stupidity to trust the man, it was still the only way.

"I've got him in my sights," Danny whispered across the narrow passage. "I can nail him."

Ethan shook his head. "No, he might take her down with him."

"Come ahead," Ethan said loud enough for his voice to carry to the outlaw holding onto Rona. "No one's going to stop you."

Dead silence filled the mine in reply. Reo didn't explode as Ethan had expected. Harding plainly was weighing the situation before replying. The quiet settled. Ethan could almost hear the steady, rhythmic breathing of each individual inside that grim chamber as seconds slid swiftly past. Then, suddenly, a soft scraping sounded from near Harding's position, and the torch that could only have been that of Sam Reo was abruptly extinguished. The lighting in the man-made cave dimmed to a creamy glow, darkening the entrance to the chamber.

Harding cursed from behind the discarded equipment. "I warned you about him. You get him off my back or watch her go down right now!"

Ethan should have known that Reo wouldn't take the direct route. He glanced around the limited area, surprised he could see nothing of Harding's nemesis.

"Back off, Reo. Do it, or you won't see a dime of that reward money. I hired on to see to Rona's safety, and that's what I aim to do. I'll blow you away myself if he hurts her."

Torregrossa knew Reo wasn't going to think much of his threats, but he had to stall, play for time, say what Harding wanted to hear.

"Hear me, Reo. I'm gunning for you. It's not just Harding now. It's me, too. Show yourself once this is over, and I'll blow you to kingdom come."

The quiet remained undisturbed, and Ethan set down the torch he had carried into the mine, slipping inside the chamber. He had learned to like the dark since the sight in his one eye had been impaired. It evened things up some.

Danny stayed with Karl, crouched just outside the cavern opening, the sights of his rifle still trained on the piece of Harding he could distinguish from Rona. If the worst happened, Danny with his eagle eye might very well be the best chance they would have at keeping Rona alive, and Ethan was glad the kid was there.

Torregrossa's nerves tightened, strung with the tension of barbed wire on a post. He was inside the room now, and it was uncomfortably small. With shock, he realized the icy detachment that had previously preceded him into a like situation was gone, irretrievably. He was no longer an outsider wielding a gun as Hank Burr — a man without illusions — had hired him to be. He hoped Hank hadn't made a mistake in sending for him. He felt a closeness, an emotion he didn't understand, for Rona. He had trained himself to feel little over a lifetime of hurt. It would take time to understand the feelings newly awakened within him. He cared what happened to Rona, but there was something more, and he didn't have the time to examine it further.

Slipping along the shored-up wall of the ancient shaft, Reo appeared in the dim, half light, a gliding phantom, little more than a thicker shadow off to Ethan's right. Ethan spotted him there about the same time Harding did, and he didn't even breathe for fear of revealing his position. Obviously, neither of the feuding pair had been aware of his entry into the roughly

201

rounded chamber, but it wasn't going to be a secret much longer.

Harding jerked Rona around in front of himself, using her as a shield and, at the same time, swung his weapon from where he had used it to cover the entrance as Reo's six-gun leveled for his shot. Ethan let his breath out in a hiss, causing an eye blink of hesitation.

Harding moved, shifting Rona who was struggling against his iron grip, intending her as human armor between himself and Reo's vengeful bullets. In the process he exposed himself to Ethan's gun. Torregrossa dropped, hitting the rock-hard floor on his belly as he squeezed the trigger. The gun kicked in his hand, and Danny's rifle exploded overhead in almost the same instant. The sound reverberated throughout the shaft with an incredible roar that spilled into the adjoining tunnels.

Harding's face, a moment before hard and grim in the circle of dark shadows, came apart in pain and surprise. He fell back, trying to bring his gun to bear on the closer enemy, squeezing off yet another shot whose echoes followed the roar of the double shot down the tunnels, his grip never loosening on Rona. Dying, he collapsed in a slow-motion parody of a dance across the rotting wood covering the ancient shaft, dragging Rona down with him. For the first time Rona made a sound, and it was a horrified yell of denial.

"No!"

She braced against it as Harding went down, but his grip seemed tighter in death than it had been in life. His body dropped like a rock. Rona let out a terrified scream as time, everything, condensed in on itself, and Tyler Harding's body dropped across the old wood, demolishing it with a splintering crash that blended with the fading echoes of the gunshots in a deafening crescendo. Rona was in a free fall. The fear, rising in her soul, told her she was going to die. She saw the pit she was plummeting into, the ragged, gaping, black hole Harding's body had made in the rotted planks. A fear so primal as to extend back into the distant mists of time sent her hands, arms, and feet flailing for something to hold on to. Painfully her hand struck wood, and an elbow hooked over a crossbeam. She felt the abrupt jerk at the back of her pants as Harding's dead weight dropped from behind her. Her hold was nearly torn free, and a freezing wash of some unidentifiable emotion surged over her when, miraculously, Harding's grip broke. She cringed, hearing his body crashing down below her until a distant, nauseating thud told her he had struck bottom.

She sprawled across the middle support that had caught her, sweating, aching, and listening to the ominous crack of the wood suspending her above the shaft. It shifted. She gasped, sucking in her breath and holding it until the framework stabilized again. Dirt, small pebbles, and bits of wood fell in a steady, pattering shower through the opening all around her into the shaft below. It was like the hissing of a serpent far below, waiting for her to descend into its maw.

"Steady, Rona," Torregrossa said quickly.

"He fell down the shaft," Reo snarled. "He fell! Now how the hell are we gonna get his body out of there?"

Forced to shift her grip, Rona groaned as the old crossbeam creaked beneath her weight.

Easing toward her, ignoring Reo, Ethan froze. "Don't move. Don't even breathe if you don't have to."

All around the chamber, even the uprights, shoring the wall in place, creaked, groaned, and gave off loud pops of disintegrating wood, loosing small streams of dry earth from nearly every overhead support in response to the vibrations set up by the shooting. For a heartbeat no one in the chamber was capable of moving. There was an eerie fascination in that moment. Second by second, the shaft's interior was dissolving away. Timbers continued to creak and moan, shifting with abrupt suddenness and considerable force, releasing even heavier floods of sandy earth to spill down.

Rona drew a very deep breath and let it out slowly, giving an odd, whispery cadence to her words. "Hurry. Just please hurry."

Stuffing his still smoking six-gun into his holster, Ethan broke the spell, easing down on his belly to crawl forward, dragging himself by his elbows to the edge of the ragged square of blackness above which Rona was dangling. She was suspended above the abyss by only three rapidly deteriorating crossbeams that had not gone down with the rest of the old wood and Tyler Harding.

"By all that's holy, Rona, just don't move until I can get a grip on you."

"He's right," Karl echoed Ethan as he crept forward with lamps and torches for more light. "Keep it steady, girl. We're gonna get you out."

"Maybe we better get a rope," Danny suggested. "Toss it to her."

"We don't have time, and the weight of the rope, hitting the timber, could be enough to send it down."

"Oh, God," Rona murmured.

Danny dropped to the floor, following Ethan's example and belly-crawled in her direction, extending the stock of the rifle toward her. She grasped it eagerly, but it provided little more than an illusion of safety.

Ethan stared at the wooden square of broken boards by which Rona hung suspended in the middle and knew he wasn't going to be able to reach her across the unstable expanse without help. He glanced over his shoulder at Karl.

"Grab my legs and hold on."

Reo stood idly by while Danny continued to brace the rifle,

attempting to give Rona something to hang onto if the rapidly failing braces beneath her gave way. Ethan squirmed out onto what was no support at all, aware of open space just below his belly and the splintered wood while Karl held determinedly onto his legs.

"Reach out for my hand," Ethan told her, "nice and easy. Just let go of those timbers and reach for me very gently."

"It's all right," Danny lied in a firm voice, holding her eyes with his own across what remained of the timbers.

"Come on, girl," Karl urged. "Take his hand."

The timbers shifted again, suddenly. Rona, trembling, gave a little cry as the wood cracked like a gunshot beneath her, then dropped her abruptly several more inches into the gaping mouth of the shaft.

"Christ, Rona, there's no other way. Grab on and be quick about it." Ethan spoke softly, but the words were clipped and anxious. "Just do it. Stick your hand out, and let me take it."

Afraid so much as to move her head sideways to see Ethan, reaching out for her, Rona, breathing in quick little gasps that dried her lips to parchment, slowly extended her free hand. Torregrossa edged his way forward a couple more dangerous inches and closed his hand about her slender wrist. He squeezed tight, hoping to give her the courage to do what she had to do next. He felt the cold clamminess of her hand as it closed about his wrist. Ethan breathed a sigh of relief. He could hold her now if the timbers went suddenly. But would Karl be able to hold *him?*

"Now turn loose of Danny's rifle, and take my other hand."

"I can't. I'll fall."

"If you *don't,* you'll fall."

Licking dry lips in terror, Rona slowly relinquished her

grasp on the warmed wood of Danny's rifle stock, turning with painful slowness toward Ethan. All around them the beams continued to creak and groan. Sand and lumps of earth continued to sift down from above as their time was rapidly running out.

Danny quickly laid his rifle aside and bent to give Karl a hand as Ethan caught Rona's other hand and began drawing her slowly toward him, backing on raw elbows across the splintering wood he'd edged out onto. Ethan was continuing to draw her in when a rotten timber broke through, plummeting down the shaft until it hit bottom with a splintering crash that sparked another round of cracking, popping, and moaning in the chamber all around them. Ethan hung on to her for dear life, sweating.

For long, agonizing seconds Rona hung free, dangling in space, Ethan's hands locked around her wrists, her own smaller hands clutching at his, while Ethan's muscles, screaming in protest at the brutal jolt, strained to adjust. Then Ethan started dragging her up by the sheer strength in his arms.

Ethan inched back away from the black hole, and Danny rushed forward, reaching over into open space to grab Rona by the upper arms, helping to pull her up over the edge. Karl never gave up his grip on Ethan's legs until they were all lying, gasping, on the dusty floor of the old mine chamber.

Reo approached and relit his torch, as unruffled and unconcerned as if he were out for an evening's entertainment at some bawdy house or saloon. He leaned toward the abyss, took a look down, then uttered a soft curse. "You've got her out of the way now. So how're we gonna get Harding's body out of there? I'll need the body to collect the reward."

"You're not," Karl snapped, accent thickening with his agitation. "Rona could've been killed, and him" — he spat in the general direction of the abandoned shaft — "he ain't worth nothing. We've got to get out. The wood will not hold. It is why I do not use dynamite in here."

He turned and started walking briskly for the exit.

Ethan quickly drew Rona to her feet, shepherding her away from the old shaft, falling in behind Karl as, from the depths of the mine cracks and pops were followed by long, drawn-out shrieks of old wood long beyond its ability to withstand stress.

"Damn you, Torregrossa!" Reo roared. "I spent two years of my life pursuing Tyler Harding. Now I'm going to collect that ten thousand, and you're gonna help me do it. It's your bullet that put him down there. It's your hands'll bring him up."

Ethan half turned, his hand still resting on Rona's shoulder and found himself staring down Reo's gun barrel. Ethan's tone was icy as he gently eased Rona away from him and out of the line of fire. Distant timbers groaned loudly.

"What do you think that'll get you?"

Danny's rifle clicked sharply as he cocked it.

"A bullet in the back," Danny promised before Reo could make a reply.

Reo's face reddened, and he appeared far from ready to back down when a loud, moaning shriek of wood turned into a rending crash as one of the timbers on the far side of the dusky chamber gave way. The collapse sent a rumble echoing through the honeycomb of passages, shaking the earth under their feet. The roar died down but the silence, collecting in its wake, sent a thick vibration through the air. For a moment none of them moved. Then Karl's prophetic words rang with truth as everything started folding up on itself, one main beam after another, tumbling in the old shaft, dirt, released from years of imprisonment, following in a wave.

"Sweet Jesus!" Karl yelled. "Cave in! Run!"

Dust billowed up around them in a smothering cloud, nearly

extinguishing their light as Reo's threat and Danny's counter-threat were forgotten in the face of the more imminent danger to them all.

Karl turned back for just an instant, grabbing Rona's hand, and then he started to run, holding his torch aloft to light the way. There had been other mine cave-ins, and experience taught that, once it started, the only safe place was outside the mine.

Ethan, Danny, and Reo were moving fast, close on the spry, old man's heels as the collapse gained momentum, a roar from deep in the belly of the mine warning there was more to come. Dirt rained down on their heads, stones dropped from the earthen ceiling, and, for the moment, Reo forgot the force that had driven him so far. All that mattered now was getting out alive. He wasn't about to come this far just to end up as dead as Tyler Harding.

Dust swirled, thickened, and choked them as their footsteps pounded against the hard-packed floor of the mine's passage, and the roar of devastation swept behind them into the main passage, tearing out newer, stronger beams in ever faster succession. The whole mountain shook and rumbled around them, driving them on.

Without letup they ran, passing an adjoining fork in the passage, coughing, choking, and gasping for fresh air, the sounds of utter destruction finally falling farther behind with each unsteady stride. They didn't slow their pace until they passed the first fork and a draft of cool, fresh air washed over them from the bright opening, looming ahead. Then Karl slowed only slightly before he led the way to the pool of daylight, and they all dashed out.

Ethan drew a deep, cleansing breath, one filled with the freshness of the pines and the coolness of the air. The mountain was still rumbling, dust now pouring from the mouth of the mine, but he relaxed, knowing they were safe. Then he started to descend the slope in the wake of Rona, the old man, and Danny.

Reo had come out last, and he didn't care much for looking at everybody's back. When he spoke, his words rang out sharply.

"Hold it right there, Hawk! You and I have some business that needs finishing."

"The name's Ethan Torregrossa. Go see your brother," Ethan said, continuing down the slope without turning around. "He'd probably like that, though God knows why."

"You're going to have to see the sheriff in town, all of you!" Reo bellowed. "You owe me! You tell him who Tyler Harding was, and he'll believe you."

Eyes red from the dust and lit by a fanatical light, Reo raved down at them from the slope.

Ethan turned, half expecting Reo to be holding a gun on him, registering mild surprise when he saw the man was empty handed.

"I don't know who Harding was," Torregrossa pointed out. "All I ever had was your word. Besides," he added with deadly calm, "it's none of my affair." Ethan stared hard at Reo, a mocking smile tugging gently at the corners of his lips.

Reo's face grew dark. "Your gun put him down that shaft. I would've had him, if you hadn't interfered and stopped me from doing it my way. I ought to kill you where you stand." His long-fingered hand hovered near his gun.

Ethan tensed, his blue eyes boring into Reo's. Danny half turned, rifle coming up. Then Reo eased up, his hard face creasing into a taunting smile that reflected the fanatic's fire burning in the depths of his slate-gray eyes. Not for an instant did he fear Ethan Torregrossa. There were better ways to handle a matter like this. And he had time. Plenty of time.

"I ain't gonna kill you, now. That would be too easy." His gun hand relaxed, and he crossed his hands over his chest. "No, I think there's a better way. Bet a man like you has a poster out on him somewhere. I'm going to find it, and then I'm going to track you down like I did Harding. You look for me. You do that from now on and wonder when I'll show up. And when I do, when I take you down, don't go thinking it'll be in a fair fight. I'll shoot you down from cover, collect that bounty, and we'll be square."

Without another word, Reo turned, striding purposefully across the dip the cabin occupied to retrieve Harding's horse from the brush beyond the corral and start back down the old mine road.

"*Is* there a poster out on you somewhere?" Rona asked Ethan.

He shrugged. "A couple. But they're old ones."

Chapter Twenty-Three

The streets of Stillwater were quiet this morning. Not much was stirring besides some town dogs and a few early risers. Ethan and Danny had spent the night in the Burr Stage and Freight office after returning to town from the mine with Rona. Karl had remained up on the mountain, business as usual with his small operation. It was going to take him some time to dig out and start working his way back into the newer tunnels.

Harding's horse had been tied to a hitching post outside the sheriff's office when they had ridden into town, Rona sharing Ethan's horse. Reo was wasting no time in making good his threat to find a dodger on Torregrossa. No doubt he was going through the sheriff's file of wanted posters. Rona had seemed worried, but Ethan took it philosophically. If Reo came after him, he would kill the man. It was as simple as that.

Danny cast a glance down the street in the direction of the sheriff's office from where he stood, looking out the window.

"You reckon he's figurin' on pulling something soon?"

Ethan looked disinterested. "Just have to wait and see. No point in worrying about it none."

He leaned back in his chair and wondered about Rona. About what she was going to do now. There was nothing left of the Burr Stage and Freight Line. No way to keep it going even if she wanted to, which Ethan seriously doubted. The future was something Ethan had, in the past, given very little thought to. That attitude, however, had become extremely impractical in recent days. Life itself had grown much more complicated since he had altered his course in mid-stream. The old ways had seemed easier when he had been living them; now they were uncomfortable. It was as though they had belonged to a strange, dark man other than himself. Ethan had given some brief thought to asking Rona if she cared to ride along with him and Danny when they pulled out of Stillwater, but couldn't decide himself if it was such a good idea. He didn't need anyone to point out that both he and Danny were dangerous men to be caught riding with. And that was without the added threat of Sam Reo. Still, he reasoned, Rona had nothing. She would have to start over somewhere, and if he read her right, she would be leaving Stillwater soon. He'd like to see she got where she was going safely. She was the kind of woman who'd want to look ahead, not back. He had already discussed the matter with Danny, and the kid was all for it. He'd have to talk to her about her plans before they pulled out.

"I'm hungry enough to eat almost anything that comes my way," Danny announced, breaking into Ethan's thoughts.

Rona strode in from the back, grinning at Danny. "So am I. I'll put something on."

Ethan climbed to his feet, boot heels hitting the floorboards with a solid thump. "Never mind. Come on, we'll go see if the hotel cook has anything to crow about. On me."

He opened the door, allowing both Rona and Danny to pass through before him, and he followed them out. They had not taken two steps into the dusty street when Sam Reo separated himself from the shadow in the doorway of the sheriff's office. By the smirk on the man's face, Ethan was figuring on trouble, and he took precautions. Without altering

212

their course for the hotel restaurant, he made sure Rona was clear of his gun hand and kept moving.

Danny glanced Reo's way and tensed. He'd left his rifle in the office, but he had his six-gun at his hip. He glanced up and down the street for any indication Reo wasn't alone and found none.

Reo stepped off the boardwalk to intercept them. When he stopped, dust rising in puffs from beneath his feet, Reo smiled sweetly, touching his hat brim to Rona. Rona pulled back.

"Found something mighty interesting when I was going through the sheriff's most recent posters," Reo said without preamble, his eyes shifting continually between Ethan and Danny. "Yep, real interestin'."

"Get away from here, Rona," Ethan said out of the corner of his mouth.

Rona didn't move.

"Might be best, ma'am," Reo agreed with uncustomary courtesy.

"I'm not sure it is." Rona didn't know what was happening, but it smacked of blood and death. Ethan had always known what he had been doing before, but he'd saved her life. She couldn't help but feel protective toward him. All the symptoms of gun trouble were passing between the two men.

Danny's hand drifted toward the six-gun riding at his hip. "Rona," he said practically, "you ain't got a gun. You stay here, you'll get somebody killed."

Torregrossa nodded, then flicked Danny a glance. "This is mine," he said quietly, as Rona grudgingly withdrew. "Maybe you better join her."

Danny was about to issue his protest, but Reo cut him off short.

"Don't be so noble, Hawk. Is that the handle you use to put the fear of God in folks? No, it ain't you I'm after. It's

213

that kid partner of yours." He held up a copy of the poster Danny's stepfather had put out on him for their inspection.

"Thousand dollars the paper says. I'll just call it a down payment on what you owe me."

"Don't push it, Reo," Ethan said, the ice flowing in his veins.

"Reckon that makes it my fight," Danny broke in between the two men.

"That's right, kid," Reo smirked. "You and me. Unless you want to come along peaceable. The poster does say alive, but I guess it'll pay off dead just as well."

Reo was none too sure about his last remark, but he was willing to risk it. He could aim low if the kid was foolish enough to try him. He'd seen Danny with the rifle. With the rifle he was deadly, but with a hand gun there was room for error.

Ethan swore. He kept his eyes on Reo. "He's baiting you, Danny. And you're falling for it."

Danny gave a nervous laugh. He, too, kept his eyes on Reo. "And you weren't?"

"It's the boy I'm calling out," Reo reiterated, remaining firm. "You either come with me now, or make your stand."

Danny wished for the weight of his rifle in his hand. He had fought before. He figured by now he'd seen the elephant, but never had it been like this. Sweat was misting his forehead, and the hand hovering near his holster felt unnaturally stiff. Against a man like Reo he had to make the first move, but his arms and hands felt like tree limbs, unbendable and stiff.

"Let go of it, Danny. Back off," he could hear Ethan saying beside him. Then Danny heard Reo laugh, and suddenly the tightness drained away. He felt loose, like he had broken free of some unrecognized restraint, and there was no man on earth who could best him.

"What the hell's going on here?" Sheriff Samovic demanded cuttingly, bursting through Danny's almost suicidal euphoria.

"Boy's wanted," Reo snapped, furious at the interruption, certain he'd seen the kid's decision to make his move stamped across his young features only seconds before.

The sheriff eyed Danny for a moment. Reo held the poster out for inspection, and the sheriff snatched the piece of paper from his hand. He wasn't a man who enjoyed having his breakfast disturbed, and, when a panic-stricken boy had called him, claiming there was going to be a gun fight in the street, he had felt no charity for either side.

"Ain't wanted no more," the sheriff growled. "Man who put that poster out is dead. Wasn't nothing to it to begin with. No law put that flier out. Nobody's gonna pay no thousand dollars now that he's dead."

"What the hell you trying to pull here, Sheriff?" Reo demanded.

"Nothing. The kid's damned stepdad put out that flier. Since there wasn't no other family members, fact is, the kid probably has the whole damned spread to go back to." The sheriff snorted and jerked the spotted napkin off his shirt front. "I told you to check with me before you went traipsing off with one of those posters, didn't I? If you'd've asked me, I would have showed you the notice I got a couple of weeks back. It's in my office. Come see for yourselves, all of you."

Together they went to the jail and stepped inside. The sheriff, rummaging through a stack of papers on the corner of his desk, pulled one out, and tossed the crisp paper across the desk to Reo.

"Here it is. Now, if this kid has the sense not to draw down on you and you plug him, I'm going to have to arrest you for murder."

New anger flared in Reo's eyes. He hesitated, looking from

one person to another in the small room. Hatred couldn't be more palpable if it were thick cheese and could be sliced. "All right," his eyes shifted to Ethan. "You win this round, but you keep watching for me, 'cause I won't be far behind."

He slammed his fist down on the desk, the paper crumpled in it, leaving it there to uncurl, then pushed past Rona, and stormed into the street. He didn't stop there, but mounted what used to be Harding's horse, and rode out.

"Well, I'll be damned," Danny muttered in awe, hardly noticing Reo's exit. "That old bastard bought it, did he?"

"Didn't have no heirs, either. At least, they couldn't find none. You're all that's left of a family, and you get the whole bag of beans. You might be a wealthy man."

"I'm just a rancher, and I might have a war to fight to take it back from those rannihans what worked for the old son. They never were hands as much as they were gunmen." Danny looked at Ethan. "You going to come with me to sort things out, partner?"

Ethan's first inclination was to say no, as he would have in the past to such an offer, but he brushed the impulse aside and nodded. "Be obliged, Danny."

"There must be nearly ten thousand acres in that spread," Danny calculated, "probably more. Plenty room for you, too, Rona, until you get settled, I mean."

"There's nothing for me here," Rona said directly. "And I don't think I've ever had a better offer. Count me in."

"Don't give a damn where you go," the sheriff growled, "just so you get the hell out of my town."

"Mind if we have breakfast first, Sheriff?" Ethan asked sarcastically.

"No," the lawman snapped. "Just be sure you haul your tails out of here right after. Excuse me, ma'am," he touched

216

his hat brim to Rona before he turned on his heel and left.

"Nothing to hold us here," Ethan called after him as the sheriff hurried back across the street to finish what was left of his cold meal.

About the Author

P(eggy) A(nne) Bechko was born in South Haven, Michigan. When young, she always loved the American West and visited it frequently. She wrote her first Western, THE NIGHT OF THE FLAMING GUNS, at the age of twenty-two. She signed the manuscript P. A. Bechko, so it came as a surprise when her agent, who had never before spoken to her, telephoned to say that Doubleday had made an offer on it. Her editor at Doubleday was no less surprised when he saw her full legal name. However, he went on to buy four more Western novels from her.

In 1981 Bechko finally moved to where she wanted most to be, Santa Fé, New Mexico. Together with her mother and with occasional help from her brother, she went about completing from the ground up much of the home in which she lives. In addition to two original paperback Westerns for Pinnacle Books, Bechko also branched out in the 1980s to write romance novels for Harlequin, but with an authentic Western setting, such as her recent historical romance, CLOUD DANCER (1991). Her books, beginning with her Westerns, have been translated into the principal European languages, including French, German, Italian, Spanish, and Dutch. Western fiction by P. A. Bechko is now being made available for the first time in Eastern Europe. C. L. Sonnichsen writing in El Paso Times described Bechko as "one of the few women in the business but she outdoes many of her male counterparts in fertility of imagination." DISCIPLE OF THE GUN is P. A. Bechko's next **Five Star Western**.